To
Albert Davis
from
Tommy Fulton
Dec. 25/30

WESTY MARTIN
IN THE ROCKIES

HIS WARM BLOOD SEEMED TO TURN INTO AN ICE-LIKE
SUBSTANCE.

Westy Martin in the Rockies.   *Frontispiece—(Page 133)*

WESTY MARTIN IN THE ROCKIES

BY
PERCY KEESE FITZHUGH

Author of

THE TOM SLADE BOOKS
THE ROY BLAKELEY BOOKS
THE PEE-WEE HARRIS BOOKS

ILLUSTRATED BY
RICHARD A. HOLBERG

PUBLISHED WITH THE APPROVAL OF
THE BOY SCOUTS OF AMERICA

GROSSET & DUNLAP
PUBLISHERS : : NEW YORK

Made in the United States of America

CONTENTS

WESTY MARTIN IN THE ROCKIES

CHAPTER I

A SURE AIM

WESTY MARTIN sat speechless in utter consternation. He glanced about him as if dazed. He seemed to be trying to make sure that he was awake, that the whole thing was not a dream. Then a sudden burst of shouting and applause recalled him to the reality of the clamorous scene.

The scene was very real. It was a familiar scene at Temple Camp and real with the savory realities of clam chowder and hunter's stew and crullers piled high in tin dishpans. And waffles built into miniature skyscrapers and big glass pitchers full of sirup and honey. And Pee-wee Harris shouting, "I'll go with you, I'll go with you, I'll be the one!" And Uncle Jeb Rushmore sitting at the head of the "eats board" with a smile of amusement hovering under his drooping white mustache.

Uncle Jeb Rushmore was one of those men who looked out of place at a dining table, even at a rustic "eats board." By all the rules he should have eaten his meals squatting on the ground in proximity to a campfire, in the dense wilderness or on the prairie. He should never have eaten a meal without his trusty rifle by his side and without a keen eye on the lookout for stealthy Indians. He should certainly never have been waited on by a smiling negro connected with the cooking shack of a great modern camp. He should have dined in remote fastnesses, mountain passes, and in sound of the appalling voices of savage beasts. Everything about Uncle Jeb suggested not the covered table, but the covered wagon. He was an old western trapper and guide who had cooked bear's meat with Buffalo Bill and fried his venison on silent trails while the caravan waited.

That this picturesque old member of a race that has all but passed away should be sitting at the head of a camp "eats board" was the fault of Mr. John Temple, the beneficent founder of Temple Camp in the Catskills. And so Westy Martin, scout, became identified with a series of adventures which I shall

chronicle for you; adventures in the wildest region
of the Wild West. Such adventures as boys do not
even read of in these days of football and baseball
and boarding schools and Saturday hikes. It is odd,
when you come to think of it, how things happen.
That Westy Martin should participate in adventures
which in these days are commonly thought too ex-
travagant even for boy's stories! Yet this thing happened and it should be told. If the worst that can be
said about it is that it is a wild-west story I will
gladly bear the responsibility of telling it to my
young friends.

To go back to where I started—they were having
dinner at Temple Camp. It was Labor Day and
soon the camp would close for the season. Mr. John
Temple, was its guest, as he usually was just before
the season closed. He was standing at the head of
the main "eats board" and it was something which
he had just said in the course of his remarks that
had set Westy Martin aghast. There were three
of these "eats boards" in a vast open pavilion. The
middle one was larger than the two that flanked it,
and it was at the head of this large, rustic table that
the guest of honor had been seated. At the head of
Westy's table sat Uncle Jeb in his accustomed place.

And at the head of the other sat Mr. Bronson, resident trustee. Somewhat removed from these three enormous dining boards was another rough table for scoutmasters. In that great scout community some troops cooked their own meals near their cabins, but all were crowded in the "eats" pavilion on this memorable day in honor of the distinguished visitor.

"And now one word more," said Mr. Temple. "It is both good news and bad news. Those of you who come next summer will not see Uncle Jeb." Murmurs of surprise and apprehension greeted this announcement. "Uncle Jeb is going home, not to stay, but to visit for a season his beloved Montana and his old cabin, those scenes which I took him from to bring him here. I think you will all agree—our trustees have already agreed—that Uncle Jeb is entitled to visit his old home. He expects to return here next fall or, at the latest, early the following spring. He has said that he will do that, and as you know Uncle Jeb always hits the mark. He aims to be back with you after next summer and I never heard anybody ever say that he missed his aim." This remark was greeted with laughter and applause.

"There is one thing more," said Mr. Temple. "It has been thought that Uncle Jeb's sojourn might afford a couple of our scouts an opportunity to visit the woolly West; I mean the regular West with all its wool on; the West that Uncle Jeb knows and which he once showed me. Uncle Jeb himself seems to like that idea. So I suggested that he be asked to choose one of the boys he knows best to go with him, and that this fortunate boy be permitted to choose a comrade in the great adventure. Uncle Jeb has named Westy Martin of the First Bridgeboro Troop of Bridgeboro, New Jersey. Westy Martin," Mr. Temple added, glancing about, "wherever you are, I congratulate you."

"There he is, third from the end, eating a waffle!" thundered the uproarious voice of Pee-wee Harris, "and I'll be the one to go with him!"

So you see how it was. Uncle Jeb was seven years older than when he had come to cast the glow of pioneer and western romance over Temple Camp. But his eye was just as keen and his aim was just as true as in the days when he had hunted grizzlies and struck terror to Indians in his beloved Rockies. For those keen gray eyes had seen Westy Martin and picked him out and knocked him clean off his feet, in a way of speaking. . . .

CHAPTER II

WHEN Mr. John Temple conceived the big scout community which came to be known the country over as Temple Camp, he had an inspiration that showed his fine understanding of the scout idea.

He decided to introduce into the camp something which neither the solemn woods nor the tranquil lake could give it; something which all the projected rustic architecture could not supply. And that was an atmosphere.

He was resolved that the scouts who flocked to the sequestered lakeside resort should live in proximity to a real scout, one who had lived the sort of life that is commemorated by scouting.

He would bring the prairies and the Rockies and the long, winding trails, and all the associations which cluster about Indians and grizzlies and buffaloes to Temple Camp in the romantic person of an old western scout and guide whom he had met while in the Far West on railroad business. Old Jeb Rush-

more had guided Mr. Temple and a party of surveyors to a pass in the mountains following what
he called a trail which was about as discernible to
Mr. Temple as a trail left by an airplane. The
founder of the camp had spent a night in Rushmore's
lonely cabin in Montana and had heard the voice of
a grizzly in the distance.

A year later when land had been bought for the
big camp in the Catskills, Mr. Temple recalled that
his old guide had told him that he expected soon to
give up his cabin in the Rockies and end his days
at Fort Benton in his beloved Montana. "Reckon
I'm gettin' old," he had told Mr. Temple. "That's
one thing yer can't shoot," he had added. Indeed
old age was the only foe that had a ghost of a chance
of stealing up on him.

So Mr. Temple invited Jeb Rushmore to come
and live at Temple Camp and the old scout, after
some hesitation, agreed to do so. He spent one
night at the magnificent Temple residence in Bridgeboro where he seemed not the least bit embarrassed
by the gorgeous surroundings. He smoked his pipe
in Mr. Temple's library and when that gentleman
related how he had gone to Washington once to seek
an audience with President Roosevelt, Jeb Rushmore

casually remarked that he and Roosevelt had hunted together in the Rockies. It developed that Mr. Temple had tried to see Roosevelt and failed and that Roosevelt had gone a couple of hundred miles out of his way to get in touch with Jeb. It was not likely that Uncle Jeb would be dazzled by the formality of Mr. Temple's household.

Uncle Jeb, as he came to be known at camp, was given the title of manager. But he had no executive duties. He was more than the camp's manager, he was its spirit. I have seen a scout camp with a statue of an old pioneer on the camp grounds to convey the idea of scouting and outdoor life. But Uncle Jeb was the living embodiment of all these things; he wore a halo of tradition. It was a fine inspiration of Mr. Temple's, bringing this old scout to camp.

Uncle Jeb built log cabins and made trails and instructed the scouts in pathfinding and stalking. He taught them the Indian trail marks. He would send a boy off to go where he would in the forest, give him half an hour's head start, then take a party of boys and find him. He did this without the least trouble.

"Why didn't yer double on yer trail?" he would

demand of the astonished fugitive after running him down. "What'd I tell yer 'bout not steppin' on no twigs 'n' bustin' 'em?"

"You can't run without breaking twigs," the embarrassed boy would protest. "And anyway, if I doubled on my trail you'd trace me anyway; so what's the use?"

"Yer don't hev ter tech no trees, do yer?" the old guide would say, " 'n' leave all yer duds hangin' on 'em like a ole wash hangin' out."

"You can't run in the woods without touching trees or even stepping on twigs," the poor victim would protest. "Anyway, it's no use trying to get away, not from you, *Jiminy Christopher!*"

What Uncle Jeb meant when he charged an unfortunate scout with leaving his duds hanging on trees "like a ole wash" was that the baffled youngster had left one strand of a fringe from his scout scarf on some obscure bramble bush.

"If yer decorate yer path like if a parade wuz comin' 'tain' no chore findin' yer, now is it?" Uncle Jeb would ask. "Here yer scares away a turtle what was settin' on a rock and I sees where the spot wuz he was a settin' on. Yer ain't reckonin' I was blind, wuz yer?"

No, they didn't think he was blind, they thought he had eyes all over him. It was disheartening trying to get away from Uncle Jeb.

"Now, youngster, you try agin," the old man would say, " 'n' remember you ain't diggin' a cut fer a railroad 'n' yer ain't layin' out no line o' march 's if yer wuz marchin' through Georgie. 'N' don't make a noise like yer wuz shoutin' the battle cry of freedom. 'Cause yer jes' scare the birds 'n' the turtles 'n' they goes 'n' tells on yer. Now you try once more."

But it would be just the same thing over again.

CHAPTER III

GOOD MAN FRIDAY

THE scouts liked to be with Uncle Jeb and help
him, but they shared these enjoyments with other
diversions, rowing, swimming, and visits to Leeds
and Catskills where they conducted masterly assaults
upon ice-cream parlors and frankfurter stands, and
satiated themselves with movies.

But Westy Martin stuck and became Uncle Jeb's
right-hand man. A score of enthusiastic scouts
would help in the starting of a new cabin. But only
Westy would remain till it was finished. A clamorous throng would start blazing a trail back into the
mountains and for the first mile or two there would
be more scouts to do the blazing than there were trees
to be blazed. But at the point of destination it often
happened that Uncle Jeb and Westy were the only
survivors.

During this very summer, of which we have witnessed almost the final scene, Uncle Jeb was engaged

in making a continuous trail around the lake. This involved the building of log fords across inlets and a rough bridge at one point. The mountainside across the lake from camp was dense and precipitous and here the making of a real path was laborious. The gang of volunteer workers soon petered out, leaving only Westy and Uncle Jeb to fell the trees and pry up rocks. All the camp idolized Uncle Jeb, but Westy was his good man Friday.

So it was natural enough that Uncle Jeb should select Westy to accompany him on his visit to the old cabin in the Rockies, which had been his home, or rather headquarters, for so many years. And it was natural enough, too, that Westy (being the boy he was) had never dreamed of being chosen for this great adventure. Mr. Temple's announcement struck him dumb.

It is significant, I think, that the first thought which entered Westy's mind upon hearing Mr. Temple's sensational announcement, was the thought of how his father would react to these tidings of great joy. He hoped that Mr. John Temple, who could do all things, would carry his interest to the point of interceding in the Martin stronghold in Bridgeboro. Sunshine had burst upon Westy and dazzled him.

And then there was a shadow, a shadow of misgiving and apprehension.

But late as it was in the season something was yet to happen at Temple Camp destined to have an important bearing on Westy's future adventures. There was one boy in his troop, who occasionally accompanied him and Uncle Jeb in their work of carving out this long-needed and circuitous trail. This was Artie Van Arlen, leader of the Raven Patrol in his own troop. He was tall and likable and intelligent, a real patrol leader. His patrol was more than a group, it was a well-conducted organization. And he had made it so.

Unlike many of the camp group, Artie had not set out to help and then grown tired of it and plunged into other diversions. Sometimes, when he felt like it, he would go across the lake and spend a day on the steep mountainside helping Uncle Jeb and Westy. He never said that he would surely be there the following day. He did not seem to consider his status as that of a helper, though he did help. He frequently rowed or paddled across at noontime with hot lunch for the two steady toilers, and often on such occasions he would remain, clearing away brush and prying rocks out of the projected path. Uncle

Jeb liked him and found it pleasant when he took it into his head to hike around or row across.

Artie was rather amused at Westy's constancy to this arduous labor. But that was the kind of boy Westy was. He worshiped at the shrine of Uncle Jeb and was a model of devotion to his hero. Dogs of certain breeds are said to recognize but one master and companion. Westy was of that exclusive and devoted type. He renounced the camp life to be with this keen-eyed old hickory nut of the plains and the Rockies. Uncle Jeb could hardly have thought of any one else to make the trip to Montana with him.

It was a day or two after Mr. Temple's bombshell at the big "feed" in his honor that Artie rowed across the lake at noontime with some bean soup and hot muffins for the trail makers. They always took a snack with them and these luscious supplements to their cold lunch came as pleasant surprises.

CHAPTER IV

THE CAPTIVE

IF it was natural that Uncle Jeb should have selected Westy to accompany him to Montana, it seemed quite as natural that Westy should select Artie to be his companion on the big adventure. At camp it was taken for granted that he would do this, not only because Artie was in Westy's troop and the two were pals, but because Artie was often with Uncle Jeb, and was serviceable to him in many ways. He was a frequent if not a steady helper.

Since work on the new trail had progressed to the opposite side of the lake from camp, the toilers saw much of him. They would hear the steady clink of oarlocks as the boat approached the shore and then Artie's voice calling from below, "Are you hungry up there? Any big rocks that you can't handle? If so, say the word; now's your chance." Then he would come scrambling up, all out of breath, to where the work was going on. They enjoyed his visits. Everybody liked Artie.

On this occasion he tied the boat (it was impossible to draw it up because the shore was so precipitous) and started scrambling up with the pail of soup to where the trail was being cut along the lower reaches of the mountain. A narrow and irregular shelf of land was being utilized to carry the trail through this precipitous area.

"How's she coming?" Artie asked. "Here's some soup; I nearly spilled it. There's a boxful of muffins down in the boat—hot ones."

"I'll go down and get them," Westy said; "you sit down and rest. What you been doing all morning? I thought we'd see you sooner."

"Oh, swimming and playing basketball and reading," said Artie. "Boy, but you're getting along, hey?"

"I'll say so," said Westy. "What were you reading?"

"Oh, a book."

Westy laughed. "That's a wise crack. What kind of a book?"

" 'Winning of the West,' by Roosevelt," said Artie, with a slight suggestion of embarrassment. "It's in the camp library. I just happened to pick one of the volumes up. That's so, when you write to me from the Rockies, I'll know what you're writing about."

"Maybe I won't write you," said Westy rather mysteriously.

Uncle Jeb winked at Artie and all three laughed; Artie's laughter had that faint suggestion of embarrassment in it that had been discernible when he mentioned the subject of the book he had been reading. The fact is that Westy had every intention of asking Artie to share his great adventure with him, but he had said nothing about this. That was because the shadow of his father lay across the whole affair. He was a careful, thoughtful boy and he preferred not to say anything to his friend which he might have to unsay later. But just the same there was a tacit understanding (and Artie was a party to it) that these three would be the ones to visit the Far West. Perhaps Artie was a bit puzzled that Westy had not put his invitation into words. But he was just as sure of going as ever he had been sure of anything in his life.

To change the subject he laughed and said, "All right, go ahead down to the boat and get the muffins and look out you don't drop them coming up; they'll all roll back down into the lake if you do. . . . All

right to sit down on this rock?" he asked Uncle Jeb
as Westy departed.

Uncle Jeb sat down on a log and opened the
dinner pail which he usually carried with him.

"Some trail, hey?" said Artie, glancing about.

"Good 'n' plain so even boy scouts can foller it,"
said Uncle Jeb. "Westy wants street lamps onto it,
but I says no, you youngsters can shout across ter
camp if yer get lost."

"Oh, sure," said Artie, taking the gibe in good
part; "but maybe a sidewalk would be good, hey?
You like bean soup, Uncle Jeb?"

"I reckon," said the old scout.

Artie had leaned forward to pour some of the
soup into the cover of Uncle Jeb's pail when he felt a
stirring of the rock on which he was seated. It was
hardly more than a tremor, but it was followed almost immediately by a more pronounced jarring.
He thought and acted quickly. Jumping up he
hauled a small log around and got it under the rock,
thus steadying it in its precarious position on the
hillside. Uncle Jeb hauled the log on which he had
seated himself over to the rock to reënforce the prop
that Artie had jammed under it. The heavy rock

stirred, then seemed to settle against this combined support and for a few seconds did not move.

"Guess she's all right," said Artie. "I prefer another seat though."

He was looking about for a place to sit down when he happened to glance down to the lake. To his surprise Westy was sitting in the boat his body turning and wriggling; he seemed to be intent upon some physical effort.

"Are you eating all the muffins?" Artie called.

"No, but my foot's caught under this plaguy stern seat," Westy called; "it's like a blamed old woodchuck trap."

"Turn it sideways," Artie laughed.

"I did, also endways and upside down," Westy answered. "It's a puzzle. I'll manage it."

As Artie moved his position for the better enjoyment of Westy's predicament he saw that the rock which he and Uncle Jeb had wedged up was directly above the rowboat. He shuddered at this thought, but the rock seemed secure so he indulged himself in the pleasure of a few humorous taunts and bits of mirthful advice to the writhing captive. Then, suddenly, there was a crash, one of the logs went rolling down the hillside while the rock, still poised, trembled visibly. Then it moved ominously and some earth and small stones went out from beneath it, rolling away. It seemed to Artie that if he touched it or even breathed upon it, it would go crashing down to the lake. He held his breath, every nerve on edge. . . .

CHAPTER V

IT SHALL NOT PASS

"Loose the boat and push off if you can't get your foot out," Uncle Jeb called; "there's a rock——"

"I can't reach the rope," Westy shouted, not knowing his danger.

Artie did not pause to call to his friend. One fearful look at the big rock informed him that it was going down. It seemed pausing like a beast crouching, ready to spring. Frantically he ran down the hillside, stumbling, catching hold of trees, now on foot, now on hands and knees. He would do what he could do quickest, and that was to release the boat and get it out of the path of the threatening monster. So as not to lose a second's time he carried his opened scout knife between his teeth.

He was about half-way down and going backwards so as not to stumble when he beheld something which caused him to act like lightning. Evidently Uncle Jeb had been putting another support under the rock. He saw the old man jump aside and heard him shout. He saw and heard in a panic of horror and did not know what Uncle Jeb said.

Artie was not conscious of thinking at all. He saw the bowlder rocking, then saw it move and roll down a few feet and stop against a big tree. There it paused, balanced for two or three seconds. Artie saw Uncle Jeb run toward it, doubtless to try and hold it poised behind the tree. In a kind of trance he saw the old man hauling a log down to where that tree had momentarily blocked it in its crashing descent.

But Artie did not wait upon the issue of this almost hopeless project. Like a panther he was up a sapling, looking hurriedly about as he ascended, taking note of its position in relation to neighboring trees. He was so frantic with haste that he had not time to close his scout knife; he dropped it from his mouth and forgot it. Near the top of the young tree he began swinging and swaying to make it bend under his weight, but he had to climb almost to the very end of it before it would do this. Then it only bent part way over. But it split somewhere below him and let him down almost to the ground where it lay against the trunk of a larger tree.

Thus in a few short seconds, fraught with peril,

Artie had succeeded in doing just what he had hoped to do; he had laid a barrier, such as it was, across the path of the rock. Simultaneously with this lightning exploit the rock rolled aside the tree where it had caught and came crashing down against the fence which Artie had placed, as if by magic, in its path. Fortunately it had not gathered much momentum and the springy sapling bent to absorb the shock of impact, then held the bowlder fast.

The human machinery which had wrought this sudden miracle was not to be seen. Amid the sparse foliage of the prone sapling Artie writhed in agony, his right leg caught between the sapling and the trunk across which it lay. The whole weight of the nearby rock which made the sapling a sort of lever, held that torn and bleeding leg as in a vise. Beads of perspiration stood on Artie's brow from the anguish he was suffering, and his hands were clammy. He saw Uncle Jeb hurrying past him down to the shore to rescue Westy and he said not a word. Then he saw the leaves near him change color, the whole world reeled, and oblivion came to relieve the torments he was suffering.

CHAPTER VI

THE RESCUER

RELEASED from the boat Westy looked up the hillside to where Uncle Jeb pointed. There was the bowlder held fast in almost a bee-line above the boat. Its weight strained the prone tree and it loomed conspicuously thus held behind this supple barrier. It looked out of place there, almost as if a human being held it. Westy shuddered as he looked. The lightning-moving human machinery which had interposed this obstacle to the rock's descent was nowhere to be seen.

"She nigh on clipped yer," drawled Uncle Jeb.

"Where's Artie?" Westy asked.

For answer Uncle Jeb only started up the bank, Westy following silently. They found Artie lying where the prone sapling crossed the standing tree. His foot was caught as in a trap. He had brought the sapling down to this secure lodgment and it held him as securely as it held the menacing bowlder. His face was tense with pain, beads of perspiration stood upon his pale brow. He had regained consciousness and was aggravating the agony he suffered by raising his trapped body and trying to see the rock to assure himself that it was held fast.

"Oh," he said weakly, "you here—you—all right, Wes——" Then he fell back again almost fainting.

They pried the sapling away from the tree-trunk, releasing Artie's crushed foot, and as they did this the slight movement of the springy barrier gave the waiting rock the chance it wanted and it went crashing down to the shore and into the water.

That bowlder has never been seen since. Its murderous escapade ended, it became a submerged and lesser peril in the concealing waters of the lake. You had better not chug around there in the camp launch except in the company of a scout who knows where that rock lies hidden. Once it ripped open the bottom of the little sailboat. And when the wind sweeps the water you may see, even from the camp across the lake, a little spray which marks the grave of Artie's rock, as they call it. They call that spray the dancing tenderfoot though some will point it out to you as the white devil. Anyway, keep away from it if you are in a boat, for it has a jagged edge sticking up.

That rock did not terminate its brief mad career on earth without leaving a memorial of its murderous power. It crushed the rowboat into splinters as it struck the water and one of those bits of wood which drifted near to the launch that took the stricken hero and his friend across to camp, was picked up by Westy and kept as a souvenir of the near tragedy.

For a day or two it seemed that this bit of wood on which Westy carved the date of the affair might be a sad keepsake. Artie Van Arlen lay with a raging fever in the little camp hospital while the doctors considered whether the amputation of his foot would be necessary, and whether even that would save his life. But the danger which they feared as the sequel of his accident passed and in a week or two his parents, who had waited anxiously, took him home to Bridgeboro. Westy saw him lifted into Mr. John Temple's big car and saw the white face smiling wanly down at him, humorously, ruefully, as they 'lifted the bandaged foot up onto one of the small folding seats.

"Wonder how I'd look going scout pace now," Artie said.

Westy said nothing. He wished he was going back to Bridgeboro too. But that could not be for he was to help Uncle Jeb board up the cabins after the noisy throng had departed. He was looking forward to being alone for a few days with the old scout. They would talk about their big sojourn in the spring and he would ask for the hundredth time, "Are you sure there are still grizzlies there? And do you think we can start just as soon as my school closes?"

Yes, he wanted to stay for those few delightful post-season days in the deserted camp. It would be almost like the lonely life he was going to have a glimpse of in the far Rockies. *The far Rockies!* How that phrase lingered in Westy's mind! But he wanted to get in that big car and go back to Bridgeboro with his friend, his rescuer. And when the car had rolled away he felt lonesome and a little guilty, he hardly knew why. That was Westy Martin all over.

CHAPTER VII

WICKED MR. TEMPLE

WHEN Westy departed from Temple Camp leaving Uncle Jeb alone in his glory for the long winter, he was filled with thoughts of the far-off springtime which loomed up beyond the long, cheerless, intervening season of cold and waiting. He would have liked remaining in the deserted camp all winter with old Uncle Jeb and helping him with the winter "chorin'" with which the solitary old occupant always busied himself.

He burst elatedly into his home in Bridgeboro, New Jersey, on the evening before the day on which school opened, his duffel bag over his back, his face wreathed in smiles. His mother and his sister Doris had only that day returned from the mountains and their trunks cluttered the living room. There was a riot of embracing incidental to this family reunion. Ghostly sheets which had protected the upholstered furniture during the season of Mr. Martin's lonely occupancy were still in evidence and the paintings on the wall were concealed behind these uncompanionable hangings. One of the trunks stood open with part of its contents pulled out and Westy sniffed the pleasing odor of apples, those souvenirs of vacation time which nestle coyly in the corners of home-coming trunks. The disused living room, bereft of all its familiar bric-a-brac had a musty odor.

Westy sat down on an unopened trunk and poured out his tidings of great joy. "You're a nice lot, you are, never writing me anything about my big award. You didn't say anything about it in your last letter, Mom; I guess you were too busy playing tennis, Dorrie. I should worry. Some work I've done this last week, *believe me!* I suppose you know I'm going to Montana next summer with Uncle Jeb and I'm going to live in his cabin in the Rocky Mountains and you can hear eagles screeching where that cabin is; you can hear grizzlies, too. And I can choose a fellow to go with me; that's what I get for helping Uncle Jeb all summer. Have you seen Mr. Temple, Dad? He can tell you all about it. Gee williger, I told in letters and you didn't even say anything about it. Didn't you get the letter I sent you up to Mountainvale, Dorrie? Talk about mountains! Why Mountainvale is—it's—it's only——"

"I did and I think it's perfectly glorious," said Doris, aged nineteen. "You know how it is, Wes, when you're up in the country, you just never write letters."

"She has a new beau," explained Mrs. Martin.

"Oh, what I know about you, Dorrie!" Westy teased in the overflow of his joy. "I should worry about letters. Anyway, I won't be here to kid you next summer. I bet you'll be glad of that. Did you can that Arnold fellow?"

"You shouldn't talk that way," said Mrs. Martin in mild reproof. "Mr. Captroop is a very nice young man and your father likes him. He's in the brokerage business in Wall Street and he's doing very well indeed."

"He's a right sort of a young fellow," said Mr. Martin, "steady and sane."

It was evident that these remarks of Mr. and Mrs. Martin were intended rather for Dorris than for Westy.

"It's nice to think he's not insane," said Doris.

"What's his name—Claptrap?" said Westy.

"You haven't asked about your friend, Artie Van Arlen," said Mr. Martin. "He had a very narrow escape from death up at Temple Camp. And so did you, from all I hear. You didn't write us a great deal about that, Wes."

"I didn't want you to worry," said Westy, a trifle embarrassed.

The fact was that Westy had not in his letters depicted the affair of the rock in all its seriousness. Every opportunity for adventure that he had ever had had been wrenched from his father after a struggle in which Doris had boldly championed her brother and poor Mrs. Martin had been his gentler ally.

Mr. Martin believed in people, even young people, being "steady and sane" and he seemed forever haunted by the thought that scouting was something in which boys broke their necks and that camps were places where they contracted typhoid fever. You could not pry those ideas out of Mr. Martin's head with a crowbar. It was for this reason that poor Westy always skimmed lightly over his adventures and related the doings at Temple Camp with cautious reticence. But he might have known that the news of Artie's mishap would reach Bridgeboro before him.

"Well, my boy," said Mr. Martin, sensing the cause of his son's reticence and speaking mildly in consideration of the boy's homecoming, "I think you should have told us the whole story."

"I don't see what Artie's accident has to do with Wes's going out to Montana," said Doris. "It wasn't a case of telling the whole story at all; they are two different stories."

"Well, then, I don't see why he didn't tell both of them," said Mr. Martin. "The Van Arlen boy had a close call from death while in company of this old man. From all I can gather Wes had a pretty narrow escape too—helping this old man. And this is the very same old man that Mr. Temple wants Wes to go off to the four corners of the earth with and risk his neck. It's very easy for Mr. John Temple to arrange for other people's sons' fighting Indians and all such nonsense and breaking their necks into the bargain. Mr. John Temple has no son of his own. Why, I thought all this dime novel hocus-pocus was put on the shelf long ago. Now here is Mr. John Temple filling boys' minds with all such nonsense and sending them off with some old fire-eater to the frontier of nowhere. The man's phil-anthropy has gone to his head. Here you are all home again, not three hours in the house, and Wes talking about going to some cabin or other out West next summer when he ought to be thinking about school to-morrow morning. What boy is he going to take with him, I'd like to know?"

"I made up my mind. It's Artie," said Westy timidly.

"Oh, I'm so glad," said Doris; "he deserves it, for his heroism."

"Well, that isn't the way to reward him," said Mr. Martin.

"You might give him a lollypop," said Doris, winking at Westy.

"Well," said Mrs. Martin, putting her arm about poor Westy and speaking in her gentle way, "we're not going to quarrel about next summer the very first evening we're all together and have so much to tell each other; we're just going to forget all about it, dearie."

"I'll tell you one thing," exploded Mr. Martin, speaking to Westy, but *at* his daughter. "If Archie Captroop had gone shooting buffaloes when he was sixteen and got his head filled up with all this wild-west business he wouldn't be drawing forty dollars a week at Ketchem and Skinners in Wall Street now. There was none of this falderal when he was sixteen, and look at him now."

"Picture him hunting buffaloes," Doris exploded mirthfully.

"Do you mean I can't go then?" said Westy.

"I mean you should settle down to school now," said his father not unkindly, "and forget everything else."

Mr. Martin was not as good a scout as his son. Westy was steeled then and there to hear the worst. But Mr. Martin had not the courage to tell him the worst. He would hem and haw and bluster all winter. But he had no intention of letting Westy go. He would talk about boys breaking their necks until the household would be weary of hearing him. By such talk he would take all the pleasure of going from Westy. Westy's hope and spirit would be broken instead of his neck. That was the way Mr. Martin worked.

CHAPTER VIII

WHAT MIGHT HAVE BEEN

THE Martins, notwithstanding their moderate prosperity, kept no car. Because people broke their necks with cars. Likewise, notwithstanding their moderate prosperity, Westy was not going to go to college. Because he wanted to go in for football and in that way boys broke their necks. Mr. Martin was not a bad sort of man, he was just (as Doris said) impossible.

The first summer that Westy went to Temple Camp a solemn promise had been extorted from him that he would not go on the water. Adventure, particularly big adventure with moderate risks, did not fit into Mr. Martin's scheme of life. He called Tom Slade a daredevil. He was certainly not opposed to the moral side of scouting, he subscribed to all the scout virtues. But the adventurous side he could not contemplate calmly. He did not believe in boys going away from home. His idea of young manhood was embodied in the person of Mr. Archibald Captroop.

Mr. Archibald Captroop was twenty-four and he never went without his rubbers when it rained. There was a young man for you! He did not sport negligee khaki and go without a hat as Tom did. He worked in Wall Street and commuted and earned forty dollars a week. He lived in Raleigh Park about five miles from Bridgeboro so it was something of a coincidence that Doris and her mother had met him at Mountainvale during the summer. Doris had played tennis with him. After the return of the Martins to Bridgeboro, Archibald proved a frequent caller, making the journey to and from Raleigh Park by the trolley. That was one thing Mr. Martin liked about him, he had no automobile.

Archibald had no attraction for Westy. He was pleasant enough and not unmanly, but he was a smug little business man before his time. Mr. Martin approved of his saving his money instead of buying a Ford and he liked him immensely. He thought that Tom Slade, assistant at Temple Camp, might take a lesson from this steady young commuter. Mr. Martin could not believe that helping to manage a camp was really a business. The idea that a man

could be a scout and guide in the silent places and
call it a business was preposterous.   To him old
Uncle Jeb was a dubious character who had carried
a gun, but never really had a business.

On his way home from school the next day Westy
stopped up at the Van Arlen place. Artie was limp-
ing about, but getting better, though he was not to
return to school for a week or so.

"I came to see you the first thing," Westy said;
"I'm on my way home from school."

"I don't have to go, thanks to you," Artie said
with his pleasant smile.

"Yes, I hear you say so," Westy answered.   "A
lot you have to thank me for.   It looks even as if
I can't pay you back like I meant to do."

"Pay me back?   Did you have a good time up
there alone with Uncle Jeb?   I was thinking about
you alone up there.   I bet it was nice just the pair
of you.   Two's a company, hey?   I couldn't do much
else beside sit and read, so I was thinking of you."

"What were you reading?" Westy asked.

"Oh, wild-west stuff."

"Listen, Artie," Westy said.   "I'll tell you now
that you were the one I was going to ask to go out
West with me.   I guess you know that, don't you?"

"How should I know it?"

"Well, you just didn't let yourself think of it, but anyway, you were the one. The only reason why I didn't say anything about it up at camp was because —well, you know how my father is. I was kind of afraid all the time that maybe he'd say nix and I wanted for you not to be disappointed. I kind of didn't let *myself* think of it till I got back, but all the while I was a little sort of shaky about what he'd say."

"What did he say?" Artie asked.

"Oh, he's just sort of begun to say I can't go; I know how it'll be. It's all off and I suppose I have to write to Uncle Jeb. Dad says your folks wouldn't let you go either after what happened to you."

"Oh, yes, they would," Artie laughed; "they'd be glad to get rid of me, I guess. My father said when I—— He said how a soldier——"

"Yes, what did he say when you—— You asked him if you could go in case I asked you, now didn't you?"

"Well, yes, I did," Artie said, embarrassed, but still amused at himself.

"So you wanted me to ask you, you old——"

"Don't hit me on the foot," Artie laughed, as

Westy's arm was raised in good-humored menace; "any place except on the foot."

"Yes, and what about the soldier?"

"The soldier? Oh, yes, my father said there was a soldier who got wounded in eleven places and he was in six hospitals in France and he was gassed besides, and he got over all that and when he got home he slipped on the back steps and broke his neck. My father said it's just as bad to break your neck in one part of the country as another. That's what Pee-wee calls logic, hey? No, gee whiz, my father would be glad to see me go, my mother too. I know the cook would."

"That's what my father's always saying about breaking my neck," Westy said. "He let me go to Yellowstone that time because it was the Rotary Club and they're all business men. But he thinks Uncle Jeb is some old bandit, I guess. Anyway, it's all off, Art; he didn't exactly say so, but I can see it coming. Only I just wanted to tell you that you were going to be the one to go with me. Now that I know what's what I can tell you."

"That's all right, Wes," Artie said. "As long as you tell me that I'll admit I wanted to go. But I wouldn't go unless you did, that's sure. We should worry, hey? Gee, it'll seem funny up at Temple Camp next summer without Uncle Jeb there. How's school anyway? Is Grouchy Gordon teaching the fourth grade yet?"

"Sure, and Four-eyes is teaching drawing yet, too."

"I thought she was going to get married," said Artie, carefully changing his position on the porch swing seat so as not to hurt his foot. "False alarm, I guess, hey? Don't move, there's plenty of room, only I have to be careful of my plaguy foot."

"Seen any of the fellows in the troop yet?" said Wes.

CHAPTER IX

FRIENDS

WESTY drew his legs up onto the seat, careful not to touch Artie's bandaged foot. And so these two friends sat one at either end of the seat facing each other and chatting. Artie was the one boy in all the troop whom it was impossible to quarrel with. He had almost a girl's delicacy and an amiability that made him likeable to every one.

"Yes, but you wanted to go all right," said Westy.

"What you don't get you don't miss," Artie said.

"Well, I'm going to miss it," said Westy sullenly.

"Well, what do you say we both miss it together?" said Artie. "Then we'll have some fun missing it. I dare say my mother will be disappointed; she's getting postcards from me out there already. Well, let's see. You were asking if I've seen any of the troop. Elsie Harris sent me up some jelly; the chauffeur brought it; I guess she wouldn't trust Peewee. Safety first, hey? Sure, all the troop have been up. Mary Temple was here yesterday; she's in Barnard now. Say, Wes, do you know how Mr. Temple first got hold of Uncle Jeb."

"Sure, he was out in Montana."

"Yes, but do you know how he got in with him? Mary was telling me about it."

"They were surveying or something, weren't they?"

"Sure, they were surveying for a branch of a railroad through a pass in the mountains. Mr. Temple himself went out there when they got to the pass because he wanted to see that place with his own eyes. *Boy,* but it must be lonely out there!" Artie burst out laughing at the solemn stare of interest and disappointment on Westy's face. "Wait till you hear what I'm going to tell you," Artie added.

"You only make it worse," Westy said.

"I had to laugh at the way Mary Temple shuddered when she told me about it," said Artie, still laughing.

"Yes, and you wanted to go out there just as much as I did," Westy said. "Go on, what did Mary tell you?"

"I've got you interested, hey?"

"Will you go on and tell me?"

"Sure, but I can't tell you the whole thing, because it's a mystery."

"Yes, go on."

"All right," said Artie, "one, two, three, *go*. Mr. Temple went out to Montana to see the pass; it was all like a deep ravine through the mountains. That's the Continental Divide out there. From there if you don't look out you go rolling down into the Pacific Ocean, *kersplash*."

"Will you talk sense and go on?" Westy fairly pleaded.

Artie craned his neck under the swing seat and glanced inquiringly here and there. "Your father isn't anywhere around, is he? Because there's a peach of a place for breaking your neck out there. Well, Mr. Temple went out there——"

"You said that four times."

Artie continued, "He went to a large city with a population of thirty-two people in it—and two dogs. I think there was a cat too——"

"Will you *please*——"

"The name of it is Eagle City; I guess it's named after the Eagle Scout Award, hey? All right, I'll go on. Mr. Temple went there, there's a train stops there every Tuesday and a week from Friday——"

"You're worse than Roy Blakeley," said Westy.

"All right, he went to Eagle City," said Artie, pursuing his narrative more seriously. "That was as near as he could get to the pass by railroad. That's where he first met Uncle Jeb. Uncle Jeb was buying tobacco at the village store and Mr. Temple wanted somebody to guide him up to the pass; I guess it was about fifty miles. They told Mr. Temple that Uncle Jeb was an old trapper and a guide and a lot of things like that. That's how Mr. Temple got in with Uncle Jeb. Uncle Jeb said his cabin was up toward the pass, somewhere up that way, so anyway it wouldn't be out of his way if he guided Mr. Temple to where he wanted to go."

"Did Mary tell you that?"

"Sure she did," said Artie, "and there must be some reason why nobody at Temple Camp knows anything about it. Anyway, I never heard Mr. Temple or Uncle Jeb say anything, did you? So then Uncle Jeb guided Mr. Temple up into the mountains—oh, but it was wild and lonely! They stopped at Uncle Jeb's cabin, just where you and I were going to go——"

"Yes, go on," urged Westy.

"Then they went on up to the pass, but they couldn't find the surveyors anywhere. Uncle Jeb found marks that showed they had been there and he showed them to Mr. Temple. He found little holes in the ground that showed where one of those surveyors' instruments had stood, and they found footprints, and a place where a campfire had been, and a place where a tent rope had been around a tree— gee, I guess Uncle Jeb didn't miss anything. They kept following the pass where it led through the mountains and they found more signs, remains of fires and all like that, but they never found the surveyors and those surveyors were never heard of again—not to this day. Tell your father that!"

Westy stared. "You mean they never got any news about them at all, *ever?*"

"And there's something else too," said Artie.

CHAPTER X

BUT Mary Temple did not reveal to Artie the full details of this tragic story. There was something about the expression on her father's face that had always lingered in her memory; an expression so fraught with anxiety and keen disappointment, that a lapse of ten years had not obliterated the impression one bit.

She was quite young then but she had not forgotten her father's evident apprehension for those lost men.

Her mother then told her in full how it had all happened and what a financial loss it had been to the railroad with which Mr. Temple was connected. It meant a terrific loss to him at the time, being one of the largest stockholders, but being the man he was he took his loss cheerfully, seeming to be more concerned with the surveyors' disappearance, than with his own losses.

So it happened that no one but the Temple family and Uncle Jeb Rushmore knew the true details of this unsolved mystery.

It seems that Mr. Temple undertook this trip to Eagle City for the sole purpose of looking over this mountain pass, that was to give way to modern engineering and serve its end as a branch line for the railroad.

The surveyors had secured a sort of agreement from one Ezra Knapp, a farmer, whose property ran parallel to Mr. Temple's and which he wanted to procure so that the thing could be accomplished by extending the branch line through the distant pass and so on down the ravine.

After the agreement had entered their possession the surveyors' wired Mr. Temple for one of his representatives to come without delay and close the contract.

He decided then to go himself, not only for the benefit of his fellow-stockholders but for his own personal satisfaction.

Arriving at Eagle City, he found to his dismay that there wasn't any hotel in the immediate vicinity.

The station agent directed him to the general store about procuring some conveyance to ride in to the

Inn, which was about fifteen miles distant and on the way to Eagle Pass, which was Mr. Temple's destination.

As he was strolling over leisurely, amusedly observing the quaint hitching posts outside, his attention was arrested by a picturesque figure emerging from the store.

Mr. Temple stood contemplating this young-old man, who was in the act of lighting a pipe as unusual looking as himself.

He judged him to be about sixty years of age, as his face was deeply lined, although he realized one could not tell definitely about that either, as the carriage and raiment of this strange figure bespoke the fact that he was ostensibly a trapper or guide and the outdoor life would in itself line his face indelibly, as a sequence of his continuous battle with the elements.

His hair was snowy white and two shrewd eyes of deep blue twinkled out from under heavy brows and lashes. A drooping mustache of pure white also marked a vivid contrast to his brown, leatherlike skin. Withal there was a vivacity and good humor about him that was undeniably contagious.

Looking up he saw Mr. Temple standing there

watching him and with a genial smile of welcome on his face walked over.

"I take it yure a stranger in these parts!" he said, cordially shaking Mr. Temple's hand.

"Yes, I am indeed," Mr. Temple returned. "And with whom, may I ask, is it my good fortune to speak?"

"Me?" he asked, his face wreathed with the light of the noonday sun. "Why, I'm probably what you Easterners call Old Timer." He chuckled softly to himself.

"Well, well," Mr. Temple said laughingly. "Surely such an individual as you, should bear a name more in keeping with yourself."

"Yes, yes," he laughed heartily this time. "I wuz born to the name of Jeremiah Rushmore and they call me Jeb for short. All the folks hereabouts has allus called me Uncle. I'm Uncle to everybody and yit I hev'n't one relative in the world," he concluded.

"That, I should think," Mr. Temple remarked, "is rather a mark of respect."

"I s'pose so, stranger," he said more soberly, and then: "Who may you be, sir?" he asked respectfully.

Mr. Temple then proceeded to tell him, and of the nature of his visit and how he wanted a guide to take him through the pass. He also told him that he wanted to get the agreement from his surveyors so that he could close the deal with Ezra Knapp.

"Wa-al," drawled Uncle Jeb, "I can guide yuh to whar yuh want ter go, fer I wuz jest on my way up to the Inn to take a look-in on my ol' pardner afore goin' home. So, you might jes as well come along with me, Mr. Temple."

And that was the way that Mr. Temple met Uncle Jeb Rushmore.

CHAPTER XI

THE LOST AGREEMENT

Mr. Temple jogged along with Uncle Jeb in a dilapidated buckboard, oblivious of any discomfort, for he was fascinated with this old scout's quaint views of life, and listened attentively to the reminiscences of his trapping days.

"Don't do much else now but chore aroun'," he said rather sadly. "Guess I'm a-gittin' too old!"

"Not at all," Mr. Temple reassured him.

"Wa-al, anyway I'm a figgerin' on givin' up my cabin one of these days," he said. " 'Tain't jest the thing when a man gits so old ter live by himself, and my cabin's pretty fur frum the Inn."

"I'd very much like to see it," Mr. Temple remarked.

"Wa-al, sir, yure shure are welcome ter come and stay a piece with me."

"That's very kind, but I couldn't stay but one night with you."

"I'm right glad to hev yuh and I'll take yuh up and bring yer back so yer kin git to Ezry's place after."

By that time they had arrived at the Inn.

The next morning they started before sun-up, just Mr. Temple and Uncle Jeb, on foot, of course. The trail began at the foot of the mountain just back of the Inn. Along toward ten o'clock they came in sight of Eagle Pass, where the surveyors had met Uncle Jeb the week previous when he was on his way down to Eagle City.

"Said they'd be here when I come back this way," he remarked, "but I guess they hevn't been able to git as fur as this yit."

"I suppose not," Mr. Temple said. "You don't think by any chance we have missed them?"

"No, indeed," replied Uncle Jeb. "Thar's not a track o' them anywhere's!"

They finally came to a spot where a lake could be seen in the distance lying right in the center of the mountains.

Looking up, Mr. Temple noted two cliffs identical in appearance on either side of the lake.

"Twin Cliffs, I calls 'em," explained Uncle Jeb. "Jes' like twins excep' thet the one has a hollow underneath. Regular nestin' place fer eagles in the winter and sometimes in the summer. Durn good place to keep away frum."

"I suppose so," Mr. Temple agreed.

Suddenly Uncle Jeb's eyes were fixed intently on the ground.

Then he pointed.

There was nothing so startling that Mr. Temple could see but a few small holes and some footprints here and there. Also, some blackened embers, evidently the remnants of campfires long since dead, that had been blown hither and thither by the mischievous summer breezes.

"What," Mr. Temple asked, "would that signify?"

"Them surveyors," Uncle Jeb replied with a rueful shake of his head. "They come as fur as here and they didn't go back and they didn't go on."

He was now gazing significantly up a trail that led up to the hollow that he had previously pointed out.

"Do you think by any chance they were up there?" Mr. Temple asked anxiously.

"Dunno," he replied, "I warned them not ter go, I know that! Thar's been a little landslide here since I passed and thet would cover up the tracks—if thar wuz any."

Mr. Temple looked and found that parts of the trail were indeed covered with sand and rock. Becoming alarmed he turned to Uncle Jeb searchingly.

"I'm sorry, Mr. Temple," he said. "Yuh kin go up if yer want to, but I'm a-thinkin' yuh won't find nuthin."

However, Uncle Jeb led the way up the trail and, needless to say, they searched, they shouted and in a frenzy Mr. Temple rushed to a trail that ran back of the cliff, but to his distraction soon realized that it became impassable after a few feet and finally obliterated itself in the impenetrable fastnesses of the deep mountain forest.

"And so your father went on to Mr. Rushmore's cabin," said Mrs. Temple.

"Didn't he look in the hollow?" Mary breathlessly asked.

"Oh, yes, my dear."

"Did he succeed with Mr. Ezra Knapp then?"

"No, it was all futile."

"Why so, Mother?"

"He said he had changed his mind and refused to honor the agreement."

"How perfectly mean!" Mary exclaimed. "But

couldn't Father hold him to it after making such a contract?"

"Assuredly in any other case, but you see this was different."

"How so?"

"The agreement disappeared along with the surveyors!"

CHAPTER XII

AFTER leaving Artie, Westy strolled home thoughtfully in the haze of an early fall afternoon. He was thrilled beyond measure and equally despondent at the same time, over the knowledge that he would never be able to see those mountain passes where the surveyors had met their doom.

He was sorry, of course, that such a calamity had befallen those poor fellows, but there was no denying, he secretly admitted, that it added still more zest and charm than before to that haven of Paradise in the far-off Rockies.

It was certainly an Eden-like temptation to poor Westy to have heard that story, for the more he thought about it, the greater his desire became to participate in the wild life for one whole glorious summer.

Still, he realized that some great good fortune would have to wave its fairy wand over the Martin household to convince his respected father that he was able to take care of himself and come back safe from that hazardous wilderness.

"I want to go so much," Westy said half aloud, as he was mounting the steps of the house. "Gee whiz, I'd do almost anything to go."

"What were you saying?" asked Mr. Martin who had previously come home from business and was divesting himself of his topcoat and hat in the front hall. "Were you speaking to me, son?"

"No, Father," Westy respectfully answered. "I was just thinking of something."

"Well, my boy," he said firmly, "you must always do your thinking in the proper places. I noticed as I came along in the bus from the station that you barely escaped being run over. One of those foolhardy speeders came rushing along without any regard to the privacy of your thoughts. There isn't any room in the world for dreamers, especially the business world. You must quit dreaming if you ever expect to make a mark for yourself in business when you get there."

"Well, I don't expect to get there," Westy whispered to himself.

"What was that you said?" Mr. Martin asked.

"Oh, I said I don't suppose I get enough air," Westy replied, feeling absolved from his white lie immediately, when his mother came forward to greet him. She smiled knowingly at her son, thankful that he had evaded any unnecessary argument.

"Well, if you have been in school studying all afternoon it won't hurt you any. The more you study the quicker you'll get through and get to business like Mr. Captroop," Mr. Martin reminded him.

"Come now," Mrs. Martin interposed, "dinner is about ready."

Westy looked upon his mother at that moment as one might look on an angel of mercy, for she had saved him from listening to a prolonged discourse on the safe and sane business career for all young men and the many admirable qualities of the Hon. Archie Captroop.

But to Westy's dismay, the estimable Mr. Martin took up the conversation at the dinner table, where he had left off.

"As I was going to say before dinner," he began, "I think it would be a very wise plan for Westy to make the most of his next summer's vacation."

"How?" Westy hopefully asked.

"By getting something to do like most energetic boys would do, instead of running around wild the whole summer with some unknown Wild Westerner."

"But, Father," Westy, crestfallen, despairingly pleaded, "I was speaking to Art to-day and it seems that he was planning on me asking him to go. His mother and father had already given their consent."

"Really, my boy, that was quite a presumptuous thing for him to do considering that he had not yet been asked. Perhaps though, you had given him encouragement!"

"No, that's just it. I knew I wouldn't be able to go and that's why I didn't ask him."

"Then he was presuming," his father said. "Talking about the Rocky Mountains it reminds me that I was talking with Archie on my way home on the train and I was telling him about this idiotic thing that Mr. Temple had planned for you and this Rushmore man, and he thought, as I do, that it's a perfectly ridiculous idea for two such young boys as you and Artie Van Arlen to go in that wild country, accompanied only by this perfect stranger whom even Mr. Temple knows little about. Archie remarked that he thought perhaps he might take a longer vacation next summer and visit the Rockies himself. A nice, steady young man like that is well deserving of some recreation when he works as faithfully as he does the year round.

"Now," Mr. Martin continued, "if a sensible person like Captroop was to accompany you, why I might make allowances!"

"That would be better than missing it altogether, Wes," his sister Doris remarked.

"It wouldn't be fair to Artie though, after him saving my life like he did," Westy chokingly remarked.

"It would be more fair to the boy not to ask him, after what has just happened, and allow him to take any more risks in your interests. You can go if you decide wisely and ask Archie; he can look out for you best. Think it over!"

That night as Westy lay in his bed the thoughts flashed like code messages in his brain and he wondered. . . .

CHAPTER XIII

WESTY MAKES A DECISION

Two weeks had passed by and still Artie was unable to return to school. His foot was slow in mending and he still limped about painfully.

"I ought to be able to get out by spring at least," he called cheerfully to Westy, who was on his way home from school.

"Aw, don't get discouraged, Art," Westy returned feelingly, as he walked up to the Van Arlen residence and seated himself alongside of Artie in the porch swing. "You'll be out before Thanksgiving, I bet."

"Gee, I hope so anyway!" Artie doubtfully exclaimed. "Still, I'd be worse off if I was dead."

"Now you're saying something!" Westy put in, feeling a pang of conscience, for before he had reached Artie's home he was wondering how he would tell him of the proposition his father had put up to him. It wouldn't be sporting to tell him now, he thought. It would be better not to tell him at all—that is not until his foot was entirely better and by that time perhaps he would have considered the matter thoroughly and decide to the contrary.

Not that Westy had contemplated anything definite as yet. Oh, no! But he had pondered it over until he couldn't think of anything else and was at his wit's end between wanting to go and the debt he owed to Artie.

He thought as he neared home that it was a bit of luck that Artie had not brought up the subject.

That night, Mr. Martin again broached the conversation along those lines.

"Son," he said, looking straight at Westy and with decision, "you have until the end of this week to make up your mind as to whether you prefer going with Archie or staying home this summer."

"Yes, sir," replied Westy sadly.

"Archie has told me," Mr. Martin resumed, "that he will decide Sunday as to where in the West he wants to go. He's going to get some booklets from the different railroads and then he will start next week to make reservations."

"Why next week, when summer is such a long way off?" Westy queried.

"Why? Because, my dear boy, Mr. Captroop is

a very unusual young man and thoroughly conservative in everything he does. Consequently, he's not putting off until the last minute what can be done next week and, furthermore, he always makes sure of where and what he's going to do before he starts out."

"Quite a remarkable person," Mrs. Martin remarked with a hint of sarcasm in her voice.

Mother-like, Mrs. Martin resented Archie Captroop being held up as an example to her son, for his lovable romantic and non-conservative traits were the very things that endeared him to her most.

Doris Martin, who was expecting the cause of the discussion to call on her that certain Wednesday evening, entered the room.

"Well," she said, "I hope Mr. Captroop takes me somewhere this evening instead of sitting around buzzing like a stock ticker!"

"You ought to be thankful," said Mr. Martin, "that he saves his money instead of throwing it away on some senseless movie that doesn't teach you anything. My motto is never to spend your money on something that doesn't bring you a full return."

"Horrors, Father!" exclaimed Doris. "You talk like a confirmed moralist."

The door bell rang its warning of Archie's arrival, so she hurried to the door.

"Do not speak about it to-night," Mr. Martin warned Westy. "It would be more proper for you to go to his house and extend the invitation—that is, if you have decided," he added meaningly.

The strains of some popular waltz were drifting in from the living room, so Westy knew it meant that Archie Captroop would add one more dollar to his savings account that evening.

He decided to go up to his room, as his mother was busily sewing and non-committal. She was heartily in sympathy with her son, but she dared not show it.

The first book Westy picked up in his room was the one Artie had been telling about and loaned to him two weeks ago. He had not read it before, for he thought it would only be adding insult to injury and also too tempting.

But he could not resist it this particular evening with the fate of this promised adventure lying in the hollow of his hand.

In the dark silence of his room some hours later he argued the point with himself, that he couldn't have much fun with that "Claptrap" guy if he did go, for he'd probably want to sit around like some old lady and not want to do anything but read the whole time.

"Still," a little voice inside him whispered, "it's far better than staying home, isn't it?"

"I suppose that's right," Westy declared, weakening. Then feeling a little mean for giving voice to the thought he added: "I could ask Archie Saturday afternoon and I wouldn't have to say anything to Artie about it, for a while, anyway!"

So Westy made his decision.

CHAPTER XIV

VINDICATION

THE days succeeding were difficult ones for Westy's peace of mind. He even avoided passing Artie's house in the event that he would see him, and so be thwarted from his set purpose.

But Friday night came quickly and he went to bed feeling as though he was facing some terrible catastrophe on the morrow. His slumber was restless and broken throughout the night.

His mother allowing him the luxury of sleeping late on Saturday morning proved a boon to Westy on this particular day, as it prevented any meeting with his father at the breakfast table. That, he was thankful for.

Lunch time came and he ate in ominous silence. Then, as the clock ticked its way around to one o'clock and finally one thirty, he left the house with unwilling steps.

"I think you're just in time to catch the bus

Father's due on," his mother called after him, coming out on the porch.

"Archie may be on it too!" his sister Doris added, joining her mother.

"Uh huh!" muttered Westy.

"What a funereal expression, when he ought to be tickled that he got Father to relent this far," Doris remarked to her mother.

"I know, my dear, but your brother feels that it is a breach of honor to slight Artie and I'm rather in sympathy with him. Still, I suppose, one must be optimistic and think it is all for the best."

Westy had reached the corner by this time and looked down the street before turning. The bus that he was to take stopped directly opposite Artie's house, but as there was still ten minutes to the good he decided he would wait where he was until he saw the bus coming.

He kept consoling himself that it was the better way not to have to face Artie just now. Leaning against a telegraph pole, he tried to whistle softly, but the notes sounded hollow and false. Now and then he would step out into the street looking for the bus, although he knew it wasn't yet due.

At this one instance, while he was gazing down

the long, paved roadway, a figure emerged from one of the houses and limped painfully down the stone walk. Westy dared not draw back or run, as much as he would have liked to, for he knew that it was Artie, and he also knew that Artie had recognized him. There was a lump in his throat as he saw with what effort Artie was hobbling along to meet him half way. He felt despicable as he smiled to this brave pal of his, by way of greeting.

" 'Lo, Wes, old top," Artie said cheerily. "I was just going to try and make it to your house when I saw you. Wondered what happened you haven't been around. Been sick?"

"Well, y-y-yes!" Westy lied, flushing with embarrassment for doing so.

"Oh, I say, but I'm sorry! Feel better now, huh? Were you coming to see me too?"

"Yes—that is—first I was, but I didn't think I'd have time. Going to take the bus to Archie's. Invited there this afternoon," Westy said, and then to relieve the pounding around his heart: "Don't feel keen about going, though."

"I can imagine," Artie said with feeling, "but it'll do you good if you've been sick to be quiet for a while. You better cross now, Wes, I think I hear your bus coming now. See you later. Wait! Look! Whassa matter with it?"

The bus came lumbering down the street pell-mell and careened from one side to the other like a drunken man.

The two boys could see, even from a distance, that something had evidently happened to the driver, as he had slunk down in his seat and his head hung over the wheel.

The huge car was running wild!

"My Father!" Westy cried. "He's in it!"

"Maybe you can——" Artie yelled as Westy ran toward the center of the road.

"Yes, maybe I can!" Westy's voice could hardly be heard above the cries of the few pedestrians in the street and the frenzied shouts of the passengers within the bus.

Westy then gauged the distance from where he stood and then backed over to the curb. With a rush it came directly toward him, heading straight for the large elm tree at his back. He must avoid that at all costs, he thought.

The door of the bus was open, the weather still being mild; so Westy jumped blindly! Just making the step he reached across the inert form of the driver, whom he could tell at one glance was dead, grasped the emergency brake, and jamming his feet down taut and firm, stopped the car with a grinding shriek just at the edge of the curb.

There were only two faces that Westy could ever remember afterward in that near fateful bus. One was the white and trembling face of Archie Captroop, whose quivering lips revealed the fact that not only had he lost his head in that near-tragedy but also his nerve. The other face was that of his father, lying prone upon the floor, the blood streaming out of a deep gash in his scalp and entirely covering his head.

With a cry of distress Westy knelt beside him and spoke to him tenderly, but there came no answer to his earnest pleadings.

He lifted his father's head up gently and with a sob that bespoke his anguish realized at once that his father was unconscious, probably dying.

CHAPTER XV

A LIFE IN THE BALANCE

THE House of Martin during the next few hours was the scene of much anxiety and despair.

A white-capped nurse was passing in and out of the sick-room, while Westy and his sister sat on the stairway, apprehensive each time that she had come to tell them the worst.

Mrs. Martin, sitting faithfully by her husband's side, dry-eyed, seemed shaken with grief inwardly and her white face looked haunted with lost hope.

Four hours had passed and still he had not regained consciousness. The doctor was standing, silently gazing down into the darkened street. He turned back toward the bedside and Mrs. Martin, watching his mobile face intently, thought she detected the faintest glimmer of hope pass across his features.

"Another half hour will tell," he told her, "and if he lives he'll have his son to thank not only for his life, but for the half-dozen others he saved from being dashed to pieces."

The doctor, it seems, had witnessed the accident, and sang Westy's praises for many a long day after.

Archie had left to go home two hours before, saying he was too upset from the ordeal to stand the suspense of waiting. They couldn't seem to get a coherent account from him as to how Mr. Martin injured his head. He said he couldn't seem to remember, he was so excited, except that he saw him fall just as Westy jumped on the steps of the runaway bus.

So Archie went and no one cared to detain him.

Twenty minutes, then a half-hour, went by that seemed to the waiting trio like years.

The nurse, reëntering the room, took the sick man's pulse and nodded to the doctor who was standing close by.

Slowly but surely Mr. Martin opened his eyes, smiling rather wanly at his wife, who was now bending eagerly over him. She was afraid to speak lest he should fall back again into that coma.

The doctor, suspecting her fear, spoke softly. "He'll be all right now, providing he has nothing to excite him. Perfect quiet and rest will do the trick. I'll be back in a few hours!"

The nurse went out of the room with him and Mrs. Martin clasped her husband's hand in hers, fighting back the tears of joy that were continually overflowing. The door opened once again, but this time it was Doris and Westy whose youthful figures were framed in the doorway.

Mrs. Martin put her finger to her lips and motioned for them to come.

"That's all right," Mr. Martin spoke weakly. "I want to talk to that boy of mine!"

"Not now, dear," Mrs. Martin said almost pleadingly. "I'm afraid you're not quite up to it just yet."

"Rats!" he replied firmly this time. "Takes a whole lot to kill me, I guess. Westy, come here!"

"Yes, Father," said Westy, with tears brimming in his large eyes as he knelt once more by his father's side.

"My boy, you're a real he-man, do you know that?" he said, raising his hand from under the coverlet and placing it on Westy's bowed head. "I'm no end proud of you, lad!"

"M-mm," was all Westy could say.

"After what I witnessed to-day—is it still to-day?" he asked, turning his head toward the window where the shades were now drawn.

His wife nodded.

"After what I witnessed to-day," he continued, sheer gratitude inflecting his voice, "I'm quite sure that there isn't a boy alive who is any better able to take care of himself than our boy. Isn't that right, Mother?"

Mrs. Martin smiled her assent.

"And so," he went on, "the only way I can repay this modern hero of ours is to grant him the wish of his heart's desire."

"I don't wish to be repaid, Father. It was no more than I should have done," Westy said, vainly trying to conceal his embarrassment.

"Oh, no, son, that wasn't any mere duty you performed on my behalf and also the others; it was true courage, the stuff that one rarely sees displayed so splendidly. I wouldn't have believed it was in you really!"

"I've always tried to tell you that!" Mrs. Martin exclaimed with a touch of maternal pride.

"But, Father," chimed in Doris, clasping her father's other hand, "just what was it that happened to you?"

"It's not much to tell, Dorrie, it all happened so quick. Archie and I were sitting together in the back seat of the bus chatting, after we left the station. We had gone but a few blocks when I happened to notice that the driver didn't stop as we passed by River Street, and I thought it was strange, as a lady waiting there had hailed to him, but he seemed to take no notice of her. Suddenly, as I was just about to mention it to Archie, the poor fellow collapsed, and of course we were all thrown into a panic. No one seemed to know what to do to stop it, and by that time we were running wild. Then, I chanced to look ahead and there was Westy standing in the middle of the street waving his arms frantically. Naturally I forgot all else and got up out of the seat intending to start for the front of the bus. Previously we had all been seated, as the car, swerving from one side of the street to the other, prevented us from keeping on our feet. Archie, meanwhile, had been quaking with fear and I did my best to calm him, but, as I was saying, when I saw Westy I got up and Archie evidently misinterpreted my intention for he arose also. I suppose he didn't know what he was doing—panic-stricken, I guess, but he pushed me aside to try and get to the front of the bus first and in doing so knocked me backwards, throwing me against the rear window. My head must have gone clear through it, for I could hear the crash of glass and then I seemed to strike something sharp. I don't remember anything after that."

"Miss Doris Martin, a Mr. Captroop is downstairs and wishes to see you!" the nurse said, entering the room.

"If you'll be so kind, Miss Treat, will you tell him I'm not at home and that my father is doing nicely?"

"Surely, I'm only too glad to," the nurse replied, "and now if you will let Mr. Martin rest for a while, you can see him again in the morning."

"Before you go," Mr. Martin said, "I want to tell Westy that he can do as he wants to, providing he comes back next fall determined to get through school as quick as he can and get to business instead of wasting his summers hereafter."

"Do you mean, Father," Westy asked breathlessly, "that I can ask Artie? Do you mean that?"

"Something like that," Mr. Martin answered.

Westy grasped his father's hand and impetuously stooped and kissed him. Rushing out of the room and down the stairs he flung his coat and hat on in the hall and hurried to tell the news to Artie!

CHAPTER XVI

THEY'RE OFF

THERE wasn't a pair of feet on the paved sidewalks of Bridgeboro that night that stepped any lighter than Westy's. He seemed to be nearing Artie's house on air and there were a thousand tiny voices all singing inside him at once.

The night felt frosty and damp after the rather warm afternoon, but as far as Westy was concerned summer dwelt within his heart eternal.

Ringing the bell he waited, excitement and joy kindling his cheeks with radiance. Mr. Van Arlen opened the door.

"Where's Art?" he asked, stepping inside quickly.

"How is your father?" Mrs. Van Arlen called, hearing Westy's voice.

"Getting on fine," Westy answered with gladness in his voice. "Where's Art?"

"You're a fine boy, Westy," Mr. Van Arlen now remarked, as though he hadn't heard Westy's question. "I hear the bus company are going to reward you for your bravery and no doubt you'll get a medal from your troop for such heroism."

"Yeh? Has Art gone to bed?" he queried, indifferent as to what rewards or medals he might get and intent only on bearing the glad tidings to his friend.

"Here I am, Wes," Artie shouted from the living-room. "What's all the excitement?"

"Gee whiz, Art, gee whiz! Bet you can't guess?"

"Quit keeping me suspended!" Artie laughed. "What is it?"

"We're going!"

"Where?"

"Why, you dumb-bell! Where would we be going?"

"Wes! You don't mean——"

"Sure."

"Honest and truly?"

"Cross my heart'n hope to die if we're not. Father just gave his consent."

"Oh, boy, but we're two lucky guys!"

"I should say you are," Mr. Van Arlen interposed, as glad as the boys themselves.

"And say, Wes," Artie broke in again, "the doctor

told me to-night I'd get to school in two weeks. Good news comes in bunches, eh?"

"Righto! I'll go home now and write to Uncle Jeb right away."

"Sure thing."

"Well I'll be going along, Art. S'long!"

"G'night!"

The winter came and dragged along interminably for the two boys. They counted the months and talked of little else in their moments of recreation.

The months finally became counted in weeks and the weeks into days, until one morning Westy received a letter from Uncle Jeb telling them to leave Bridgeboro the following week and meet him at the Grand Central Station in New York.

The eventful day was glorious with sunshine and fragrant with the perfume of budding trees and flowers, as Westy and Artie said their final good-bys.

Mr. Martin soberly commanded Westy what to do and what not to do, but the chirping of the birds in the neighboring trees seemed to tell Westy that he could afford to listen, for there ahead of him was the thrilling promise of real adventure.

Their trip to New York was uneventful and when they arrived at the Grand Central Station, the picturesque figure of Uncle Jeb stood out individually amidst the hustling throng. His very presence seemed to breathe clean, fresh air into that artificial atmosphere.

He caught sight of the boys almost at the same time they saw him. With his familiar smile of welcome he joined them.

"Howdy, boys! I reckon now we're jest about on time. Are yuh both ready to leave?" he asked, laughing heartily.

"I'll say so!" they answered unanimously.

When the "all aboard" was called and they felt the tug of the engine making ready to pull out, Artie and Westy looked into one another's faces beamingly.

I've always thought since, it would be rather a difficult thing to decide, as to which one of the boys looked the happiest.

CHAPTER XVII

"HILLS"

THE sun was hardly more than a perceptible blur behind the vast wall of mountains surrounding Eagle City when Westy, Artie and Uncle Jeb alighted from the Pullman train onto the station platform.

They were fatigued after their long and tiresome journey and followed Uncle Jeb wearily over to a rather dilapidated looking Ford, ostensibly the only taxicab the town afforded, which was to convey them to the Inn.

The rickety little car started off with a snort as they seated themselves in the springless seat. Minus shock absorbers and all, they gave themselves up to the clear cool wind blowing gently in their faces as they sped along the rough, unpaved roads.

Time itself seemed to stand still as they flew past little unpainted shacks and makeshift abodes, for there wasn't any Super-Seven that covered the ground any faster than this rattle-box of a flivver. Here and there they would catch a glimpse of some pretentious looking ranch-owner's home, until gradually civilization was left behind and became no more than a speck on the horizon.

They were in the foothills now, with the towering Rockies on all four sides. It seemed to Westy, who was dexterously trying to keep his seat with the others, that they would surely run clean into the mountain-side whichever way the driver might turn. He confided as much to Uncle Jeb who smilingly remarked: "Got more 'n ten mile to go yit, afore we come to the Inn and after thet it's a couple more 'til we hit the trail into the hills."

It amused Westy and Artie considerably to hear Uncle Jeb refer to that majestic pile of rock and pine forests tipping against the sky-line, as the "hills."

" 'Tain't high here, boys," he said, divining their smiling silence. "Wait'll we cross Eagle Pass tomorrer, this side o' my cabin! Them's what yuh call mountains over there shure 'nough." This with a finality that did not leave the boys in any doubt as to what they were to expect.

By this time, they were swiftly approaching the picturesque little Inn that nestled with such an air of peace and contentment against the lordly mountain-side.

CHAPTER XVIII

"SILENT" OLLIE BAXTER

LATE twilight had thrown a gorgeous cloak of purple mist over the whole surrounding country as the trio of weary scouts ambled up the stone steps into the long, low room which served as a lobby, dining-room and ballroom all in one.

There were few balls or parties held in that rustic Inn except on festive occasions, such as weddings, etc., when the farm and ranch folk would gather there.

"Ol' Pop Burrows," pioneer and crony of Uncle Jeb's, who owned the place, greeted them with all the warm hospitality so characteristic of the real, honest-to-goodness Westerner.

By the time Westy and Artie, with their miscellaneous baggage, had been shown to their room, the aroma of a delicious dinner was emanating from the kitchen below them.

"Boy, but that smells good!" Westy exclaimed, in the process of washing up.

"Now, that's what I'd call an instance of mental 'telegraphy,' " Artie remarked, smiling through the folds of a face-towel.

"You mean mental telepathy," said the ever-serious Westy.

"You go to the head of the class for that," laughed Artie. "Whatever you call it, it smells good."

"Let's snap into it! I'm as hungry as the proverbial grizzly," Westy said, walking toward the door.

"You've got nothing on me and I'll be right with you, Wes."

They descended the stairs and found Uncle Jeb already awaiting them. He led them to a table at the far corner of the room where the steaming food was being placed by a little wizened-looking man, whose agile step and manner belied somewhat the immobile expression of his face.

Indeed, he was an unusual looking man; swarthy skin with "the smallest eyes." As Artie remarked, "You'd almost wonder how he could see out of them."

"Evidently, no one could say they were the windows of his soul," said Westy. "They're not big enough for a fellow to tell whether he's looking your way or not."

"Maybe he hasn't any soul," put in Artie, who afterward had good cause to remember this jesting remark.

"Now, boys," drawled Uncle Jeb, who had been eating in silent contemplation while Westy and Artie were talking, "you hain't doin' Ollie Baxter justice when yuh talk 'bout him thet way. He wouldn't hurt a flea, 'n I guess he's shure 'nough got a soul, fer he never says nuthin', jes cooks fer Ol' Pop, waits on table when them tourists come in summer, 'n does all the chores thet's asked o' him on the place. I reckon thar hain't a man livin' thet minds his bizness like Ollie Baxter; no, sir!"

"Well, pardner, I reckon yuh're dead right," chimed in Ol' Pop, as he seated himself by the table. "He came strollin' in here one day nigh onto ten year ago. He sez to me as quiet like as if he had allus known me: 'Pop,' sez he to me jes like that; 'Pop, I'm a furriner roun' these parts, 'n jes by accident I heerd down in Eagle City thet yuh wanted a man to do chores. So, I thinks to myself thinks I, I'm the man he wants, so if yuh don't mind I'll take it pronto!' Jes like thet he talked, quiet like, but to the point; nuthin' fancy."

Ol' Pop Burrows, like many of his type, manipulated his food by means of the knife with all the dexterity of an expert. As he talked between bites, he would wave the implement in mid-air, as if to express himself more fully to his interested listeners. Then, with a swoop (that would do justice to only a bird of prey), he would descend upon his plate, scoop up the proper amount that the knife would hold, and presto—it had disappeared The conversation would then be resumed.

To Artie and Westy, who were amazed at this work of ingenuity, each recurrence made them marvel more, and gave them a secret thrill to be in company with these two old scouts of the Rockies. In fact, late that night, when they were in bed and exchanging confidences, they both agreed it must have been great to have lived in those days that Uncle Jeb and Pop Burrows had lived in as boys; when mothers and fathers didn't keep tabs on a fellow's table manners and things like that.

"Just think," said Westy, "all boys had to do in those days was to fish, hunt and eat with their knives, no sisters to boss a guy around and tell you what to do as if they're your own mother."

Artie agreed to this most heartily. He also expressed his contempt of our present-day civilization in a few words that did not leave any doubt as to his feelings in the matter.

"Anyhow," remarked Artie with a ring of enthusiasm more pronounced in the darkness, "we can do as we like all summer and that's something. That is—we can do as Uncle Jeb does, I mean."

"Bet your life," said Westy. "Gee, I can hardly believe we're here, Artie, can you? Pinch yourself and see if it's true."

"Don't hafta, when I get a whiff of that ozone coming in the window. Guess the Rockies is the only place in the world where the air smells like this," Artie murmured, his voice drifting sleepily into space.

"Uh huh!" said Westy in a monotone. "Gosh, but I'm tired, ain't you, Art?"

"Sure!"

"G'night, Art!"

"Night, Wes!"

Uncle Jeb, passing by their door into his own

room, called good-night and reminded them that they were to make an early start in the morning.

They answered him drowsily and sleep must have overpowered them before the echo of their voices died away in the night. The moonlight, streaming in through the open windows on the two sleeping forms, transformed the room into a magic fairyland of dancing silver shadows, giving the whole an air of profound tranquillity.

CHAPTER XIX

UNCLE JEB SOUNDS A WARNING

BEFORE the great golden orb of light had shown itself behind the "hills," Uncle Jeb hailed the boys with a cheery good-morning.

They stretched themselves with an affected weariness and bounded out of the bed to make ready for their short journey to the cabin.

Uncle Jeb had already started to breakfast when they arrived downstairs. Ol' Pop joined them shortly and they consumed the hearty food with much gusto.

"Silent" Ollie, as Westy now called him, was hustling back and forth from the kitchen attending to the wants of the hungry quartet.

His head was sparsely covered with iron-gray hair and his thin colorless lips scarcely deviated an eighteenth of an inch from his mouth, except to answer yes or no. He was exceptionally slight of build, but still, one seemed to gather a suggestion of muscularity about him.

At all events, he was a source of interest to the two boys, notwithstanding his disinclination to talk to them.

He had come from the kitchen bearing a steaming, savory pot of coffee. At that moment, Ol' Pop Burrows was relating all the events and happenings that had taken place around while Uncle Jeb was East at Temple Camp. He remarked quite casually that he had done a "fair to middlin' " business in the little Inn that previous summer.

"Gets better every year," he said. "Expect to take in more'n ever this year; yes, sir; it gets better every year," he repeated more to himself than to his listeners.

Artie was gazing with rapt attention at this old timer, but Westy's gaze was centered on Ollie. It had been centered there ever since the conversation started, for the observing Westy had caught a faint expression of real human interest on the stony countenance of Ollie Baxter. It was barely perceptible, but Westy saw, and having seen remembered. . . .

The sun was now well out of its hiding-place behind that gigantic curtain of rock, and the dew was glistening in its crags and crevices like so many millions of precious diamonds.

THEY WERE GAZING IN AWE AND ADMIRATION AT THIS
SCENIC WONDER.

Westy Martin in the Rockies.

Uncle Jeb, Westy and Artie had bid farewell to Ol' Pop Burrows and his retinue (Ollie) and turned their steps still further westward.

Their equipage consisted of two old mules that carried their week's supply and baggage—and themselves.

The journey was not such a long one, but precipitous, Uncle Jeb informed them in his drawling manner. He led the way through narrow trails, resplendent with the verdure of late spring, sometimes ascending the craggy slopes, sometimes descending. At last, after a few hours' of steady going, they came to an open space reminding one of a deep bowl in the center, where a mountain lake peacefully reposed. Before them and behind them the mountains loomed high and imposing in their majestic serenity.

As they were gazing in awe and admiration at this scenic wonder, Uncle Jeb directed their attention high above them, where the steady flap-flap of a mountain eagle's wings sounded like the drone of an aeroplane in the distance. A terrific screech broke the quiet as another one approached—evidently its mate. They circled around high above the lake and then disappeared among the crags and fastnesses of mountain forests.

"Thar hain't a bird I know of thet I like to leave alone better 'n an eagle," said Uncle Jeb with a speculative gesture toward the spot where they had disappeared. "Right nasty customers when they're cornered, yuh kin depend on thet. Fight to the last ditch fer their young 'uns."

"Where do they nest, Uncle Jeb?" questioned Westy, his interest now thoroughly aroused.

"Wa-al," answered Uncle Jeb, "I reckon yuh cud find out soon enough if yuh set by the lake very long. I'm a-goin' to warn ye, both of ye, if yuh finds out, steer clear, or yuh'll git the worst of the bargain."

Uncle Jeb never wasted words and the boys were well aware of it, so did not ply him with idle questioning. They were both burning with curiosity to ask him of Mr. Temple's visit with him so long ago and the story of the surveyors; but they felt sure now, because of his reticence on the subject, that it must be a matter of confidence, so they left it for some more propitious occasion.

So they did not bother him with the whys and wherefores of the habits of the eagles, for they had too much respect for Uncle Jeb's knowledge of the mountains, its inhabitants and their respective habits.

His was a knowledge, so the boys contended, that far surpassed anything one could learn in school.

Westy and Artie, following Uncle Jeb around the lake and up the trail on the last lap to the cabin, walked silently and serenely, confident in the superior knowledge of Uncle Jeb Rushmore.

CHAPTER XX

WESTY MAKES A DISCOVERY

It was well along toward mid-morning, when they came in sight of Uncle Jeb's picturesque cabin almost hidden among the giant pine trees. It stood there solitary and imposing, bespeaking character, such as only one like he himself could give it.

It has often been said that a man's house is but a reproduction of his life, and nothing more true could be said of Uncle Jeb's wilderness cabin.

The door was bolted from the outside to keep away intruders of the forest, but always open to the weary stranger.

As Uncle Jeb opened the door, the boys could see at once that the place was meticulously clean, notwithstanding its long state of unoccupancy.

There were bear skins covering the floor and walls, and the furniture consisted of a table and some chairs carved out of the productive forest trees. There was a stove in the back where some wood was lying beside it, all cut and ready for use. A few pictures hanging on the walls were distinctive of the good taste of this hardy mountaineer. The most prominent of these pictures was one of the late President Roosevelt, autographed. Uncle Jeb was very proud of this and did not conceal the fact.

There were no beds in this little quaint cabin, just four bunks built along the walls like berths.

After unpacking their belongings and helping Uncle Jeb put the place in order they all set to, getting the noon-day meal with zest.

Artie stayed in the cabin peeling the potatoes, while Westy went with Uncle Jeb to fetch some water from the neighboring brook back of his place. He told Westy that this cheery little brook tinkled its silvery way down into Eagle Lake.

"More trout 'n you could ever eat in a lifetime, here in this brook, son," Uncle Jeb told Westy. "Kin hear it most any hour of the night when everything is quiet. Best company any one would want."

Westy could well believe this, for the gurgling water, plashing down the rock-ribbed mountain side on its journey to Eagle Lake, was heard quite distinctly above the chirping birds and the screeching of little forest folk even at noonday.

After lunch was over, Uncle Jeb told them they

were at liberty to do as they wanted, for it was quite late in the day to do any exploring. He promised them, however, that he would take them on a hike the following day over some all but forgotten Indian trails.

Uncle Jeb seated himself quite comfortably outside the cabin with his pipe and Artie decided he would stick around also and read.

But the restless Westy, being the true scout he was, strolled off into the forest to do a little exploring on his own.

He walked along noiselessly, striking into a trail that wound its precipitous way up through the mountains still further. Then suddenly it seemed to merge itself into another trail, one part running on down to the lake and the other part running straight up to a formidable looking cliff directly opposite the one that they had seen the eagles disappear from earlier in the day.

Looking skyward, Westy observed that the sun was on the decline, but he figured he could make the top of the cliff and get back by supper time.

After a strenuous climb he came at last to the top of the cliff that seemed to jut far out into space. Earlier in the day, when Westy had looked upwards from the lake, it had occurred to him then, that perhaps one could almost reach across from one cliff to the other. From below it really looked as though the two cliffs, jutting out on opposite sides, met in mid-air above Eagle Lake. But, as Westy scrambled out over the rocky precipice, he realized just how much the naked eye can be deceived by distance.

Sitting on an overhanging rock, he looked across and then below him. He smiled when he saw what a gap it really was that separated the two cliffs. And with a shudder as he glanced downward, he saw that he was sitting directly above the center of the lake.

"Whew," he said aloud, "that's some drop if any one should ask me. Wait'll Artie sees it from here."

Then his attention was directed elsewhere, for from the distance came that droning sound now familiar to him. Suddenly he saw an enormous eagle descending (it almost seemed to come from heaven) and heading straight for the cliff opposite.

In a second another appeared joining the first one and they both disappeared as before behind the rocky cliff.

"There," said Westy half-aloud, "is their aerie and that means we are to keep away from that cliff!"

CHAPTER XXI

THE MYSTERIOUS HOLLOW

As he came into the open clearing by Uncle Jeb's cabin, Westy could detect the smell of bacon frying crisp and brown. Uncle Jeb hailed him and good-naturedly asked if he had any trouble getting back.

"Not so's you could notice it," he retorted.

While they were eating supper he related to them his experience and discovery of the afternoon. Uncle Jeb listened intently and then cautioned the boys to be careful about going so far out on the cliff.

"Not only thet," he said, "but yuh can't allus tell when them birds'll take it into their fool heads to make a new nest on t'other side where Westy wuz."

They sat in breathless silence, as he told them many thrilling and hair-raising adventures of his boyhood days.

"What do yuh boys say we turn in now?" he concluded.

Indeed the boys did not need coaxing to turn in,

for their eyes were already heavy with weariness and want of sleep.

They tumbled into their respective berths with goodwill and soon Sleep drew her mystical curtain about them and their first night in the bosom of the Rocky Mountains.

Uncle Jeb and the boys generally made a weekly visit to the Inn. As he and Ol' Pop had much to say to one another as a rule, Artie and Westy would try to kill time by getting Ollie to talk. Between them they would hurl a veritable barrage of questions at his poor, meek-looking head, until one would imagine he would answer, if only to silence them.

Nothing, however, seemed to perturb his calm in the least. He was utterly unaware that any one was speaking at all, except for an occasional flicker of interest, visible only when Ol' Pop's name was mentioned.

On this particular early summer morning, Artie and Westy were sitting on the spacious porch reading some letters from home and many from Temple Camp, when Pop Burrows remarked he had "fetched them from town nigh onto three days ago. Could jes' as well o' let Ollie take 'em up to ye, but I thinks to meself that you'd be down afore long.

"Ollie, he generally takes hisself off for long hikes in the afternoons. Sez he never gits tired o' climbin' the hills. When he fust came, Uncle Jeb used to say as how it was durn funny, a tenderfoot like Ollie never got tired o' climbin' the hills every afternoon jes' for pleasure. Well, after thet, I kinda feels Ollie out once 'n fer all. I sez, 'Ollie, how come yer so fond of roamin' the hills every day, you thet's a tenderfoot?' 'Well,' he sez to me, 'I been brought up in de city; never outside it till I comes here, and when me woik is done I likes to go off by me lonesome with me pipe and sit quiet, that's all.' Thet's all he ever told me about hisself," continued Pop, "no more 'n no less. After thet we never bothered him and he never bothers us." He looked toward Uncle Jeb as if for verification of his story.

Uncle Jeb nodded his assent between puffs of his pipe. Then he arose quietly as Ollie came around from the back of the Inn, leading the two mules who were bearing a fresh supply of provisions for the scouts.

Taking their leave of 'Ol Pop they were soon on their way, walking single file where the trail narrowed. Presently Westy called to Artie and told him of the word he had received from home.

They also talked of the news which they had heard from Temple Camp and this Uncle Jeb listened to with interest.

Roy Blakeley wrote that, as usual, Pee-wee Harris was doing good turns; that is, he started out to do them, but rarely accomplished his purpose without a series of mishaps intervening. "At any rate," Roy concluded, "we're not a bit envious of you fellows out there (Oh, no!) so long as we have Scout Harris to disturb the calm of a hot summer's day."

Just then they came out into the clearing by Eagle Lake and Uncle Jeb suggested that they sit for a while and rest, when their eagle friends announced their advent with a series of screeches.

Instead of disappearing beyond the cliff this time, one flew into a small hollow just underneath the precipice.

Before Artie could retract his words they were out: "Isn't that where the surveyors disappeared, Uncle Jeb?"

Uncle Jeb was quiet for a while but then finally he answered softly: "Yes, my boy, 'n I always figgered somehow thet the holler is responsible. I cudn't say jes' why I do, but still thar's no tellin' 'bout them spooky lookin' places after all!"

CHAPTER XXII

SOMETHING TO THINK ABOUT

As they were nearing the cabin Artie called to Westy: "I'm looking forward," he said, "with delight to having Ollie bring our mail twice a week. We couldn't have a more pleasant visitor and I hope he comes early, so he'll have time to tell us all the news, don't you?"

"Yeh," answered Westy, "he's too talkative to suit me. I'm afraid he'll annoy Uncle Jeb's neighbors."

"They might move or even threaten to have Uncle Jeb evicted for allowing such noisy people on his premises."

"I reckon Ollie ain't sech a bad sort, boys, if I'm any jedge of human naitchur and I think I am. No one hain't ever fooled me yit, and at my age I don't think I'm likely ter be fooled. All Ollie Baxter asks in life is a good home 'n he has thet with Ol' Pop sure enough. Why, Pop hasn't a relative in the world and that's what Ollie likes about staying with him. Nobuddy to bother him."

"Well, but listen, Uncle Jeb," said Westy, his interest now thoroughly aroused. "Doesn't Ol' Pop make quite a lot of money during the summer season?"

"Yes, indeedy, son," he answered, chuckling, "and thar hain't a livin' soul knows whar he keeps it. All the folks aroun' are thet curious to know jes' what he does with his money. I even heard say thet thar are some who call him eccentric. Durn busybodies, thet's what I call sech folks. Tain't any one's affairs what he does with his money."

"Perhaps you're right," said Artie seriously, "but it may be people are afraid some harm will come to him during the long winter months, when he is alone there except for Ollie. Hoarding money is a dangerous practice. I should think he'd prefer putting it in the bank anyway so it would draw some interest for him."

"Listen to the young banker!" Westy teased. "I bet you'll never let your money get rusty in the ground!"

"Not while there's banks to put it in," Artie retorted. "Believe me, I'm no believer in this Captain Kidd stuff anyway. It always causes a lot of trouble; people even killing one another trying to find it. You always read that in books and in the end no one finds it after all."

"Who can tell but what Ol' Pop will die some day without having the chance to tell any one where it is," Westy cheerfully added.

"Tain't likely Ol' Pop will die for a long time yit," Uncle Jeb said, touched with the evident concern of the boys for his old friend. "Barrin' accident he's good fer twenty year at least, so thar's no need to worry. I spec when he gets ready he'll tell me."

"Let's hope so, anyway," Westy said as if quite willing to consign the subject to the mercy of Fate for a while.

CHAPTER XXIII

THE OBJECT ON THE CLIFF

THE days seemed to merge themselves one into the other, and, as Westy remarked, "Night did not seem to be a dividing factor in the present scheme of things at all."

Uncle Jeb built them a canoe, showing them how it was done in true Indian fashion. They launched it in Eagle Lake, with all the ceremony one would accord some palatial yacht.

One morning quite early, they set out for a swim, leaving Uncle Jeb behind whittling some wood with which to make a new bench for the cabin.

It promised to be a very warm day and Artie and Westy had no sooner arrived on the shores of the lake than they were into its cooling waters. They shouted in pure exultation, trying to outdo one another in aquatic prowess. Finally tiring of this, they clambered upon the banks to rest.

Westy had picked up a handful of pearly white pebbles that lined the shores and started skimming them across the surface of the transparent water. Artie, meanwhile, was musing thoughtfully, eyes cast overhead, when he observed the two enormous eagles emerging from their rocky fortress and almost instantly disappearing above the clouds.

Upon hearing these miniature aeroplanes "take off," Westy also followed their swift flight with an observant eye until the billowy clouds hid them from his view, thereupon resuming his pebble skipping.

Artie, however, kept his watchful eye glued upon the spot that the birds had so recently left. Perhaps it was the steadfastness of his vision; perhaps not; but Artie could all but swear to it that some small object was moving on the cliff. He rubbed his eyes, thinking it was the sun deceiving him.

Yes, he was sure of it now; something surely was moving. Without speaking, he simply gripped Westy's arm, as if fearful that his voice would break the spell. He pointed above them.

Feeling the tensity of Artie's grip upon him, Westy followed the direction of that hand in utter bewilderment.

The small object seemed to be moving on the very edge of the cliff. Now it looked to be hanging on the precipice, while the boys sat breathless—waiting.

There was a slight movement as the object revealed itself to them.

"It's an eaglet!" exclaimed Westy in an excited whisper. "Probably just trying out its wings."

"Gw-an," answered Artie, as if thoroughly informed as to the eagles and their habits. "Whatcha think, a bird that size is just trying out its wings? It's trying something you can bet on that, but that isn't any eaglet, it's too full grown."

"Well, I won't argue with you about it. I know that eaglets are pretty big birds though. I know that much!" Westy said decisively.

"It's hard to tell from here," Artie said sagaciously. "Whatever it is, I'd like to know what kind of a stunt it's trying to pull off."

"Gee, so would I," Westy said with enthusiasm.

The minutes passed and still the stately young bird clung tenaciously to the precipice. The boys decided that it must be clinging with its sharp talons to the luxuriant undergrowth that wound itself around the cliff.

They still sat in silence and watched every move. It was swaying now, swaying dizzily, as if it was losing its grip.

"Why, I wonder," Artie spoke up, "doesn't he fly?"

"Search me!"

Suddenly, then, a harsh scream pierced the air as the unfortunate bird lost its hold and dropped—into the hollow just under the precipice.

Another scream; more shrill than the one before, a scream of pain—then Eagle Pass lapsed into its usual deathlike silence.

CHAPTER XXIV

ARTIE AS A MODERN DANIEL

"WELL," said Westy, jumping to his feet, "we ought to try and save that bird. I think its wing was broken!"

"Yeah, so do I," answered Artie. "How can it be done, I ask you? Besides being dangerous, I don't think that Mother and Father Eagle would appreciate our heroic efforts to do a good turn for their progeny, should they happen to return in the meantime. Also, young Eaglet may not possess a sense of gratitude if he's still alive and kicking when we get there."

"Granting what you say is true," said Westy seriously, "if we are to live up to the scout ideal we'll have to take a chance, just so we can relieve that poor wounded creature of its suffering. Certainly it must be in agony the way it screamed! Another thing," he continued, as if by way of explaining the feasibility of his plan, "there are two of us, and while one rescues the bird the other can be on the lookout for the older birds' return."

"If you ask me which I'd rather do," said Artie with mock-seriousness, "I can tell you without a moment's hesitation."

"This isn't any time for fooling, Art!" pleaded Westy, craving action. "We've got to act, not talk."

"I got you the first time!" Artie answered good-naturedly; then: "I'll rescue the bird providing you act as lookout!"

"Well said!" replied Westy. "We'll step on it first and talk afterwards. Suppose we paddle across and save time?"

"Whatever you say, big boy!"

They paddled swiftly across the lake and landed almost at the foot of the trail to the cliff. Westy jumped out first and just as though it were agreed between them, led the way.

The trails to both cliffs were the same, going straight up from the lake like a stairway. They hurried along silently, stumbling over the loose rocks and underbrush that was more pronounced on this trail, being rarely trod upon.

Here and there, Westy noticed with his discern=

ing eye that some one lately, perhaps even the day before, had been walking up there also and descended the same way. A twig here and there had been snapped off and trampled underfoot as if in leisurely contemplation. Who, thought Westy, would be using that trail, and for what purpose? Then he reminded himself that it wasn't the time to be speculating on anything but the real object of their own presence on that forbidden trail. He deferred then to say anything to Artie of his discovery until later.

Artie, however, had not missed anything either, but kept silent and stumbled after Westy in a state of thrilled expectancy.

Approaching the edge of the cliff quite cautiously, they looked, first above and then around them. Then on their hands and knees they crawled over the jagged rocks. At last peering over the edge into the hollow, Westy could see the bird lying prone. Even with his inexperienced eye he could tell that it was a very young bird, but yet enormous. Artie was also looking and thinking the same thing. About to say so to Westy, he turned to find a very dubious expression on that young man's face.

"D'ye think you could make it, Art?" whispered Westy half fearfully. "Even though I'm shorter than you I'm pretty sure I could do it."

"Tut tut, m'lad!" answered Artie with an effort to conceal his appreciation of Westy's concern for his safety. "Sure I can make it all right. What I'm worrying about is what'll I do when I get there?"

"Why," said Westy relieved, "all you have to do is hand me the bird. It's too exhausted to show any resistance."

"Well, here goes, then," said Artie softly, making ready to swing over the ledge. "I feel like Daniel entering the lion's den!"

CHAPTER XXV

TAKING CHANCES

THE bird had fallen in such a position that it lay out on the very edge of the hollow, thus making Artie's descent less precarious.

Westy helped him over until Artie's feet pointed directly to the center. Letting himself slowly down, he landed finally with a thump, safe and sound. Taking a cautious view of his present situation, he thought it looked like a box seat in a theater, the precipice forming a protective roof overhead. One of even medium stature could not stand upright in this haven of rock, so sequestered from all the world.

"Hey, Art, make it snappy, will you?" called Westy impatiently. "This isn't the time to dream!"

Artie leaned forward and touched the inert bird with his finger. It did not move. He repeated the action to make sure. Then, he lifted it slowly, gently, and ever so cautiously with both hands, but was convinced that he had nothing whatsoever to fear from that source.

His next move was to lift the bird high enough so that Westy (who was hanging perilously over the edge with outstretched hands) could grasp it. To do this, it was necessary for him to step out on the tip end of the ledge, where there was a slight eminence. From there he thought he could reach up to Westy's dangling fingers without having to release his hold on the helpless bird at all.

Artie realized as he pondered over the wisdom of this, that one misstep meant—eternity. Holding his breath and with a firm resolve not to look out nor down, he concentrated his mind solely on his two feet. He quickly mounted the jagged edge, clasping the bird tight with both hands.

"All set?" he cried to Westy excitedly. "You'll have to grab it quick for I won't be able to keep my balance for long."

"Righto!" answered Westy, sensing the peril of both, but putting all of his courage in each of his hands, he leaned as far over as he possibly could, without throwing himself over altogether.

They both reached, but, alas, came about within three inches of making it.

"I can't, Wes, it's no use," Artie cried, "it just

can't be done!" He was feeling sick now from the suspense.

"Could you just throw it easy, Art? Try it! I won't miss it and this little distance won't hurt it any more than it has been hurt!"

"Sure—anything, so long as I get off from here."

Artie tried to steady himself once more. Then as lightly as possible he tossed it to Westy, who caught it, surprisingly gentle.

Seeing Westy slowly but surely drawing himself back again upon terra firma, Artie, with a dizziness amounting almost to nausea, stepped down from that Pinnacle of Destiny and into safety.

Unashamed, he wiped the perspiration from off his face and sat down in the hollow a minute to regain his composure.

"Well!" he called to Westy. "I'm down, but how am I going to get out?"

"What were you saying, Art?" Westy shouted from above.

Artie repeated his question.

"Why you can get out the same way as you got in, can't you?"

"Not so's you can notice it!"

"Why not?"

"Why? Just because there isn't a place for me to get a foothold on the whole darn precipice; it's just as smooth as glass."

CHAPTER XXVI

THE EAGLES' RETURN

"NEVER mind, Artie old boy," Westy said soothingly. "I'll run down and get the rope out of the canoe. Won't take me a minute! You take a rest and try and enjoy the view while I am gone. Bet the lake looks like a regular amphitheater from there, doesn't it?"

"You told it!" replied Artie. "Say though, it's a shame you didn't get the chance to come down and take a look at the amphitheater yourself. If you had told me of your curiosity, I'd have let you get the bird yourself. There's not a selfish motive in my make-up!"

"I'll say there isn't," Westy answered, glad of Artie's good humor.

"Artie!"

"What?"

"I am pretty sure I think I hear the eagles coming back!"

"Don't tell me that! You sure?"

"Yep."

"What did you do with the bird?"

"I laid it back on a rock and wrapped my scarf around it until I can see what's the trouble with it."

"You better take it and run to the lake, Wes! They're coming fast. I can see them way off."

"You don't think I'm going to let you stay here all alone, do you?" Westy fairly screamed. "What kind of a scout do you think I am, huh?"

"I'm safe enough here. You grab that bird and beat it as quick as you can. There'll be something doing if they find the bird lying there hurt and you too! Two of us can't fit in here and besides there isn't time. You run and wait by the lake until they go away again, then you can help me get out. Oh, hurry, Wes, please, they're almost here!"

Not having any other choice, Westy was spurred into action by Artie's pleading voice. He took the bird up carefully and started on a run, skillfully dodging in and out of the trees and bushes down along the trail. This he did to camouflage his presence from the two eagles, who had already descended upon the cliff.

He maneuvered his descent without discovery,

looking back from time to time to reassure himself that Artie was safe from detection.

Reaching the lake, he went over to the canoe, where they had beached it. To his dismay he found that in their excitement they had turned it over after getting out, leaving the end that had held the rope hanging over the water's edge. Consequently it had dropped out and floated away and probably by this time it was floating its merry way down into the subterranean depths of Eagle Lake.

"Can you beat that for luck?" Westy questioned aloud. "I can't paddle the darn thing across either with this bird in my hands, and I'm afraid to lay it down. I'll have to get around to the other side of the lake so I can keep my eye on Artie. I better hurry so I can tend to the poor thing. It's still alive all right; I can feel something moving."

He was out of breath between talking to himself and running, but finally he reached a spot where he could command an excellent view of the hollow. He waited a while, apprehensively. His patience was soon rewarded for he became aware of something moving within the hollow, and then perceived it was Artie waving his handkerchief to assure him of his safety.

Westy drew a deep breath, the first he had stopped to take since he had left Artie. He hated to think of having been forced to leave him up there alone.

"Gee whiz," he said aloud, as he slowly unwound his scarf from the bird, "if we hadn't stopped to fool we might have made it at that. Jimminy, I wonder?"

CHAPTER XXVII

HELP

As the scarf came slowly off, Westy gazed with awe and admiration at this ferocious, yet magnificent bird that he held within the hollow of his left arm. Tenderly he placed it down on the soft warm earth. Instantly an expression of perplexity, then amazement, appeared on his face. He stared and then bent closer.

Could it be possible, he thought? That he, Westy Martin, had so deceived himself and was so stupid as to hold the creature all this while and not know it?

"Why," he said aloud now, "I could swear I felt his heart beating!"

Then the light of reason dawned in his bewildered mind. It must have been his own heart palpitating with excitement and the exertion of running. Hadn't he held the bird close to his left breast? Of course!

"Well!" he spoke softly now, but with exasperation. "I'm the original dumb-bell! It probably was dead when Artie handed it to me! It's stone cold now! Can you beat it? And all this for nothing! As usual, poor Artie's the goat!" he murmured regretfully, looking up toward the imprisoned boy hopefully for some further sign from him.

There was none, for Artie wisely kept himself well within the enclosure, as the two eagles were now perched menacingly on the edge of the precipice.

"Can it be," thought Westy, "that they are already scenting their young one to where he had fallen?"

He felt suddenly panic-stricken as the birds, now screeching and fluttering back and forth over the cliff, seemed to be threatening something. He wondered if he should run back up there and try to fight off the birds. But the futility of the thought became apparent, when he remembered the missing rope and realized how utterly impossible it would be for him to try and fight those two enormous birds single handed. As yet, they did not seem to be aware of any intruder in their midst, so Westy decided the only course, and perhaps the wisest one, was to run back to the cabin for Uncle Jeb, while there was yet time. He figured that Artie, with luck on his side, could manage for a while at least to keep in concealment.

It would be a race against odds; but nevertheless the chance would have to be taken.

Westy's feet hardly touched the ground, as he ran impetuously onward. Yet, it occurred to him, as one so often experiences in a dream, that his legs were moving, and although he knew he must have covered quite some distance, still it seemed that he was not gaining much momentum after all.

Thinking to save time, he struck into a trail that he and Artie had explored shortly after their arrival. It was a short cut to the cabin and they had only used it a few times. He hadn't gone far when he discovered that it had become so overgrown with weeds and a maze of underbrush, that it was almost impenetrable and would retard his progress considerably.

Disgustedly he turned back, stumbling over rocks, his hands cut from brambles, his face bleeding from overhanging branches that struck him as he rushed blindly on.

Retrieving his way once more, he at last came within sight of the cabin, all the while shouting lustily for Uncle Jeb. There wasn't a sign of him inside or out, he soon realized, almost distracted. What to do next he did not know!

"Here," he thought aloud, "this isn't any way for a scout to do things! Why, I'm acting like a panicky schoolgirl. I've got to get help and get it quick!"

He decided first that Uncle Jeb couldn't have gone very far, as the shavings of the partly made bench were still lying scattered over the ground back of the cabin. That in itself was sufficient proof of his imminent return, he reasoned, because one of the many fine qualities Uncle Jeb possessed was neatness. It was characteristic of him that, despite his extremely interesting career devoted wholly to the Great Outdoors, disorder of any kind never held a place in his fine, wholesome life.

Coming around to the front of the cabin, an idea presented itself to him as he happened to glance westward. At a short distance from the clearing around the cabin, there was a decided and almost sharp break in the ground that reminded one of a sort of jumping-off place. This declined straight downward, forming a gulley running on either side of the cabin as far as the eye could see. Beyond, the mountains climbed again in their eternal race with the clouds, utterly indifferent to the yawning gulley that nature had so inconsistently cleft in their sides.

Before the idea was fully formed in his mind, Westy was going foot over foot down the rocky ladder that Mother Earth through æons of time had, in her process of reconstruction, worn away. This she had generously provided, realizing, in her infinite wisdom, the helplessness of the poor human mortal.

Reaching the bottom, Westy looked around for a second and then started his climb up the other side. Not losing a moment, he soon gained a high spot that commanded a pretty fair view of the wild country surrounding the isolated cabin.

Raising his hands to his mouth and bringing all his lung power into play, he hallooed vehemently in each direction. His voice reverberated, it seemed to him, throughout the whole United States. He thought actually five whole minutes had passed before the echo died away into nothingness.

Just as he was about to try once again, he was rewarded with a faint, almost unintelligible answer. . . .

CHAPTER XXVIII

BETWEEN TWO FIRES

EVERYTHING was silent again, and Westy waited, all the while listening intently. Then he tried it once more. This time the answer came not so clear, but louder. He recognized the voice immediately as Uncle Jeb's and it did not sound far away either.

"Where—are—you?" he called ever so slowly.

"Up—at—the—elm," came the answer, faint again.

"M'gosh!" exclaimed Westy. "The elm? The elm?" he repeated, trying to figure out where it was and what had happened. There was only one distinctive elm tree that he had heard Uncle Jeb mention, and that was a little distance above the cabin, overhanging the gulley. That must be the place, he assured himself.

That he didn't meet with disaster was nothing short of good luck, for he didn't walk or run—he fairly slid down that precipitous slope.

The elm wasn't far and, by keeping in the gulley, Westy soon reached it, not much the worse for wear. There he found Uncle Jeb lying helpless and bleeding quite profusely from a hole in his head. His foot was securely caught in an old rusty bear trap. He was not unconscious, but quite exhausted from the pain in his foot that the trap with its terrible pressure was causing. Also, Westy detected at once, he was extremely weak from loss of blood. He bandaged his head with strips of his own and Uncle Jeb's handkerchief. Then with the aid of some old sticks lying around in the gulley he finally succeeded in dislodging the old scout's foot.

In spite of his age, Uncle Jeb was no weakling and though his foot and head were throbbing with intense pain, he managed to raise himself with Westy's aid.

"Wa-al, son, so fur, so good," he said weakly. "Can't expect a young fella like yuh to act as a crutch fer me though. Yuh better get Artie!"

Helping him down on a rock so he could rest, Westy related to Uncle Jeb all the events leading up to Artie's present peril.

"Sakes alive, boy!" he exclaimed, looking up with a discerning eye on the waning sun. "Thar's not a secunt to waste fer yuh to git to the lake afore dark. As fer me, I kin take muh time and crawl back to the cabin slow. I kin make it all right!" he added, noting Westy's look of anxiety.

"Are you perfectly sure, Uncle Jeb?"

"Sure as yure a foot high," he answered with a forced cheeriness.

Westy accepted this declaration, not without a little dubiousness however. He had every reason to feel that way, for Uncle Jeb looked anything but capable of helping himself. If he was ever between two fires, he was now.

"Yuh go straight to the cabin, Westy! Take my rifle off the wall, but don't use it 'cept yuh get in a tight corner, 'n yuh'll find the rope and a lantern. I say tuh take the lantern so yuh kin signal Artie, 'n not cause I didn't think you cud find yer way back in the dark!" the old scout reassured Westy.

"I know you didn't, Uncle Jeb," Westy said, his voice quivering, and hating to leave, though he knew the time was flying.

"Go along now, boy!" Uncle Jeb commanded. He was wishing fervently that Westy would go, for his head was reeling and his mouth felt parched and therefore he was afraid lest Westy should discover his steadily weakening condition.

So Westy took his leave of Uncle Jeb with a heavy heart and climbed out of the gulley, so as not to be tempted to look back and weaken.

After Westy disappeared from view, Uncle Jeb, with much difficulty and effort, managed to get on his hands and knees. It seemed to take him an hour to crawl a few feet, his foot felt so heavy and the pain was so great. After lying face downward for a few minutes so as to rest his dizzy head he raised up a bit and to his consternation it seemed to be growing dark.

"Funny!" he said aloud, "it's a-taken me all this time to get this fur. I'm feelin' durn sleepy, I know thet much!"

But it wasn't growing dark at all—except in Uncle Jeb's fevered mind, for a merciful unconsciousness had come to his rescue and was already plunging his tortured senses into oblivion.

CHAPTER XXIX

FACE TO FACE

WHEN Artie caught sight of Westy breaking into a run up the trail, he thought intuitively that he was going for help. Instantly he was warmed with good feeling and hope that they would return soon and find a way to effect his escape. He sat silent and rigid within the hollow, for the birds had put in their appearance now, frantically strutting back and forth over the precipice, evidently searching for some trace of their lost young.

One or the other kept guard on the precipice continuously, screeching with such terrific force that Artie felt as though the echo itself would all but ruin his hearing. His muscles were stiff and sore from the cramped position he was crouching in, and not only that, but he was getting hungry. He had had nothing to eat since breakfast, but tried to cheer himself with the thought that it was better for him to be hungry, and keep quiet about it, than to let the birds in on it.

At times when the eagle was stalking on the very edge of the cliff, the sun would reflect the bird's shadow upon the jagged rock in front of him, worn smooth and glass-like with age. Then, poor Artie would sit in a state of nervous terror until the shadow had passed.

His legs were aching violently, even though they seemed to be numb when he would try and relax them. His back felt almost as if it had become brittle and would snap in two, should he get the chance to stand upright. He was beginning to doubt very much that the chance would come, for whole months had passed in those hours since Westy went out of his life. What he would give, he thought, for one glimpse of the athletic young figure swinging furiously down the trail!

His vision was becoming blurred from the strain of watching so intently from such a distance. He was beginning to fancy at times that some of the pine trees along the trail were moving a little. Then he tried to reason that the lethargic state he was in from the hours of waiting, was responsible for his double vision. He did not want to admit that his nerves were giving way under the tense strain.

The sentry on guard was still screaming at inter-

vals, and poor Artie began to think he was screeching when he wasn't, and wasn't when he was. Then
he tried to muster up his ebbing courage and with
renewed hope looked down upon the trail once more.
Surely, he thought, Westy could not be much longer!
What on earth was keeping him?

The afternoon wore on and it began to get damp
and chilly in the hollow after the sun had left.
Slowly, ever so slowly, it was withdrawing its warm
friendly rays from all about him. Then, finally, the
last lingering light that had cast sort of a farewell
shadow down upon the lake, died away and Artie
felt now that he was surely deserted and left com-
pletely alone in the unfriendly chill of near-twilight.

A dozen times he had examined the smooth rocks
over which he had slid into the hollow. Nowhere
had he found a foothold with which to brace himself over the cliff. But, as hope springs eternal and
the screeching had ceased now for quite a while,
Artie arose to a stooping position. With eager eyes
he sought once more some hidden crevice that perhaps he had overlooked. He felt cautiously of the
smooth surface and with a gesture of despair re-
signed himself to the knowledge that without help
it could not be done.

A deep silence now reigned and it gave Artie hope, thinking that perhaps the birds had given up the watch and gone back to their aerie. He stretched his aching body and getting to his feet boldly, carefully raised on his tiptoes, throwing his arms upward and running his fingers along the wall of rock. It was maddening, he thought, that his fingers couldn't grasp something! Oh, if only he were a few inches taller!

In this cogitative state of mind he heard a distinct rustle—silklike; maybe the wind. Then again —nearer. He listened intently as it came closer, and suddenly he felt something touch his fingers ever so lightly.

His warm blood seemed suddenly turned into an ice-like substance. For, peering above him, he found that he was looking directly into the face of an eagle!

CHAPTER XXX

CRIES

WHEN Westy left Uncle Jeb and started toward the cabin, he was frantically trying to dope out a plan with which to rescue Artie. A hundred and one ideas had already been half-formulated in his anxious mind, but none seemed logical when he tried to think of them being put into action.

He hadn't asked Uncle Jeb's advice, not only because he thought himself quite capable, but also because he didn't wish to overtax Uncle Jeb's needed strength by asking questions. He knew one thing, and that was, that the eagles wouldn't give up their search until dark anyway. And it was better that he should get Artie out before pitch dark and get back to the cabin.

Hurrying along with Uncle Jeb's rifle over one shoulder and the rope and lantern supported by his other arm, Westy could not help feeling a certain thrill. He felt like a real scout now, and an honest-to-goodness hunter. No one could possibly know

what a glorious feeing it really was. There wasn't
the least bit of vanity or egotism about him, but
nevertheless, just this once, he cherished a secret desire that his father, mother and sister might see him
thus.

His thoughts he did not let interfere with his
progress, for his flying feet had already outdistanced
them, as it was still quite light when he began the
last descent to the lake. The nearer he came the
more fearful he was that perhaps it would be too
late.

A half-finished prayer was still on his lips, as he
swung out of the trail by the open lake. Walking
over to the spot where he had left the dead bird, he
raised his eyes apprehensively toward the hollow.
He gasped!

There, perched on the ledge of the hollow, was an
eagle, wings spread, as if for attack!

He frantically tried to perceive if Artie was moving within, but the eagle's spread wings screened
Artie—if he was still there, alive——

"It can't be possible," he cried aloud, "that God
would be so unmerciful!" Unashamed he dashed
away the tears that were streaming down his cheeks.
His cry echoed all around in the Pass.

It must have attracted the bird's attention, for Westy could see that it had turned on the ledge of the hollow and was looking down to the spot where he was standing. Then to his great joy, he heard a cry, a human voice, almost plaintive in tone.

The eagle, evidently nonplussed, flew back to the precipice with a screech that was awful to hear.

Westy realized with a deep sense of relief that not only had he been given an inspiration, but he had also succeeded in combating the bird's purpose, whatever it was, for the time being, at least. He now emitted a cry more cogently this time and valiantly tried to imitate the eagle's screech.

It answered!

Again and again Westy would cry and each time he was rewarded with an answer. But he knew he could not waste valuable time by keeping it up. It would be dark before a half hour elapsed. Then his face brightened as his eye lighted upon the still figure lying under his scarf.

"Will it do any good?" he questioned quite loud. "I wonder! Yet, it might work at that!"

Taking the bird in his arms and screaming intermittently, as before, Westy started up the trail at breakneck speed, keeping his eye all the while on the hollow opposite and the precipice above it.

The eagle was now pacing to and fro on the ledge, giving Westy cry for cry.

It was a decidedly difficult thing for Westy to do, running up-hill at the pace he was and using his lung power to the limit besides.

By the time he reached the cliff he was exhausted. His throat was sore and he thought that perhaps when he finally got through shouting, he would certainly never be able to yell again. That, in itself, would be a tragic calamity to a scout such as Westy Martin.

CHAPTER XXXI

WESTY MAKES A SACRIFICE

QUICKLY and quietly, with a discerning eye around him, Westy picked a spot near the edge of the precipice in which to carry out his plan. At the foot of a giant tree in the moss-covered earth, with trembling but dexterous fingers, he dug into the ground, tearing away small rocks and dirt with a will that was born of strong determination.

The eagle, meanwhile, had been joined by its mate and together they screamed for vengeance, while the shadows gathered around them.

At last, apparently satisfied with the depth of the hole he had dug, Westy carefully lowered the dead bird into it, making sure it was so placed as to allow the tip-end of its wing to reach just above the top of the excavation. He then set to the task of re-filling the grave and went about it with a diligence that his frenzy for Artie's safety inspired.

Making sure there was ever so little of the bird's wing exposed, he packed the mound of earth around

it, but not too hard, and covered it high with pieces
of broken rock of a certain size, and over the whole
he placed a larger rock than those which he had
placed around the mound.

All this time the birds seemed to be holding a sort
of pow-wow as to what to do with Artie, who was
anxiously wondering what Westy's scheme would
bring about. In one breath he would mutter "good
old Wes," and in the next one he would silently be-
seech him to hurry. It was awful, he thought, the
time Westy was taking to do whatever he was at,
when in reality it had not covered the whole of ten
minutes. That one half hour of Artie's life, he
afterward recalled, seemed to have covered a span
of years. Undeniably he was no end thankful that
the bird hadn't bothered him, and he realized it was
Westy's timely return that saved him from a fate he
shuddered to think of.

Westy had managed until now to keep his presence
concealed from the ferocious birds. He wanted to;
but now that his purpose was accomplished, he stood
in full view of them, having crawled out to the edge
of the precipice on his hands and knees.

Taking out his penknife, he clenched his teeth,
and gashed several fingers on his left hand without

uttering a sound. He held his hand in such a way that the blood dripped over the ledge, and so walked back, marking a crimson trail over the gray-colored rocks, until he reached the little mound, allowing the scarlet fluid to saturate it and the earth around.

The pain from his wounded fingers was so intense and his throat felt so terribly sore when he began his cry, that his hoarse voice, plaintively reverberating through the tomblike hills and valleys, bewailed like some spectral chorus in the shadowy twilight.

The aggressive birds listened now in silence. But only for a few seconds. Their shrieks of threatening retribution that had previously been directed down to Artie's deafened ears were now transferred to the retreating Westy. He had gone down the trail a way and hid behind the protecting trunk of a large pine tree, still crying in answer to the eagle's screeches, his voice almost unintelligible now. His anxiety was soon diminished and he gave way to a sheer exultation of feeling, for the eagles had left the precipice and landed on the cliff, scenting the trail of fresh blood that Westy had sacrificed.

Moving nearer and nearer toward the mound under the tree, their cries told Westy that the search was at an end. He did not wait to see the culmination of their discovery, he glanced back only long enough to make sure they would have a long and difficult struggle to get the pile of rocks and dirt from off the uncovered wing.

Stopping long enough to wrap his scarf tightly around his hand and stem the flow of blood, Westy ran on down to the lake and continued so on up the other side to Artie's rescue.

Darkness had almost enveloped the hollow when Westy gained the precipice. Placing the lantern in such a position that he could see, he leaned over and in an inarticulate voice called Artie's name.

There was no answer.

CHAPTER XXXII

THE BOND IS SEALED

THE perspiration stood out like little particles of frost on Westy's forehead.

"What," he asked himself, "has happened?"

Had Fate inevitably overtaken Artie after all? He couldn't and just wouldn't believe it! So raising the lantern above his head he swung it over the hollow that it might penetrate every niche of it. Then peering eagerly, he caught sight of a foot sticking out from under the projecting rock. His heart felt as if it had dropped a couple of inches, for the fact that Artie was lying there prostrate was perfectly evident.

Tying the rope around the lantern as best he could, considering that his maimed hand was little or no use, he lowered it carefully into the hollow. A sound emanated from below, and to Westy, who was expecting the worst, it sounded like some one groaning.

"Whassa matter?" the voice said in guttural tones. "Haven't you got any sense? Letting the sun shine in my face like that, huh? Lot of feeling you got for a guy, I'll tell the world!"

"The Lord have mercy on us," reverently exclaimed Westy, "he's delirious!"

"Delirious, my eyebrow!" the voice, now assuredly Artie's, replied. "M'gosh, zat you, Wes?"

"Bet your life!" answered Westy, with a heartfelt sigh of deep relief. Then: "How do you feel, Art? Think you can stand being hoisted up now?"

"Say now!" replied Artie, gazing gratefully up at Westy's worried countenance. "How do you get that way? Can I stand it? Well, I guess!"

"All right then," Westy murmured dubiously, "you better keep the lantern, Art, and tie the rope around your waist. I've got the other end O.K. Think you can manage to tie it?"

"Tie it?" Artie couldn't seem to comprehend.

"Yes," said Westy and then with hesitancy, "Will you be able to, I mean!"

"Well," exclaimed Artie, "I'll be blistered! Whatcha think I am, Wes, a cripple?"

"You can bet I don't think any such thing when you can talk that way."

"That's better, Wes; but say, where are my enemies?"

"The eagles?"

"Sure! What a foolish thing to ask. Who else would I be inquiring about so solicitously?"

"I don't like to hurry you, Art, but we can't spare any more time gossiping like a couple of old ladies over a clothesline. Our friends won't be much longer in digging out their progeny. Not only that but it's imperative we get back to Uncle Jeb as quick as possible, if you feel up to it!"

There were many questions and remarks that Artie would have liked to voice at that moment, but he realized that the seriousness of Westy's tone forbade it. He told him to go ahead and tie the rope to the tree and when he felt the tug he'd start.

It was like witnessing some one arising from the dead for Westy to see the familiar form of his friend come safely over the edge of the precipice. There was joy ringing in his soul and tears in his eyes, when he saw him get to his feet and untie the rope from around his waist. Westy rushed forward and put both his hands on Artie's shoulders.

"Gee, Art!" he said chokingly, "able to stand all right and all, huh?"

"Sure," Artie answered with a catch in his voice, affected by Westy's emotion, and then to cheer him: "I'm standing all right, but I suppose I'll feel like a pretzel for the next few days, until I get the kinks out from sitting down all wound around myself."

"Same ol' Artie! Then you weren't hurt at all?"

"Hurt? When?"

"When I first called you."

"Search me! I didn't know you were there until the lantern awakened me and you said something about me being delirious."

"Awakened you? Then——"

"Sure. I must have fallen asleep. I don't remember anything after I saw those enlarged screech owls fly away. No doubt their departure affected me to the point of exhaustion."

"Well, I'll be darned!" was all Westy could say. "You've an eye for slumber, I'll say that. Come on now, old boy, we have something to do before the night is over, I'm afraid. Will you take these things from me now? Then I can walk faster."

When Westy explained to him all that had occurred since he left the lake in the afternoon, he skipped lightly over the cause of his wounded hand. That he was in pain from it, Artie could almost feel in the darkness.

"And to think that you did all that for me, Wes!" he said, intense feeling in his words. "You're the best scout that ever lived!"

They had left the lake and were going up the trail. Artie could think of no other way to express his heartfelt gratitude to this true and tried friend of his, so he put his arm out and about Westy's shoulder firmly. Silently and hurriedly they went on through the dark, deep mountain forest, feeling in their hearts that the incidents of the day had served to cement a bond between them of loyalty and everlasting friendship that nothing could sever.

With his arm still about him, Artie seemed to feel that Westy's step dragged and halted a little now and then.

"Bet you're tired, Wes, huh?"

"Just a little, Art."

The moon came out just then in all her silver splendor, lighting up the trail along their way. Artie grasped the opportunity to glance at Westy so as to smile his deep appreciation, and was dismayed to see that his face was white and his lips looked almost green in the moonlight.

Renewing his grip on Westy's shoulder, he felt his body relax against his and saw his eyes close slowly.

ARTIE HALF-CARRIED UNCLE JEB INTO THE CABIN AND
LAID HIM IN HIS BUNK.

Westy Martin in the Rockies.

Page 150

CHAPTER XXXIII

UNCLE JEB FACES A CRISIS

ARTIE realized in a moment that it was exhaustion and the loss of blood that caused Westy's faint, so he braced himself and, with a prayer for the strength to do it, he managed to get him partly over his shoulder. Leaving the rifle, lantern and rope behind, he continued on, as he knew that he needed both hands and arms now for his present burden.

Coming out into the clearing at last, he could see that the cabin was in total darkness. He was breathing laboriously under the strain of Westy's dead weight, but was supremely thankful that he had at least succeeded in getting him there safely.

Kicking the door and calling loudly, he waited a minute, but received no response from within. He then laid Westy down upon the ground tenderly. The moonlight streamed through the whole interior of the cabin as Artie opened the door. Looking around, he saw to his further consternation that Uncle Jeb had not returned.

To resuscitate Westy was his first immediate duty and then to go to Uncle Jeb's relief was his next. He lighted the lamps and, fixing the bunk, he proceeded to get Westy into it. He removed his shoes and then set to work bathing his mutilated hand. He looked with pity at those poor gashed fingers. What a sacrifice, he thought, for him to make in order to get him out of the hollow and get back to give Uncle Jeb assistance as quickly as possible. Instinct had surely warned Westy aright in this case, for the poor old scout hadn't been able to make the grade after all.

So Artie hurriedly ministered to Westy and awaited anxiously for him to regain consciousness. His eager eyes detected a slight flush gradually mounting in those white cheeks. After a little while the eyelids flickered and opened slowly. A wan smile lighted his features when he saw Artie, anxious and concerned, sitting there waiting, a glass of water in his hand.

Artie held the glass to Westy's lips, supporting his head meanwhile with his free hand.

"Feel better, huh?" Artie asked, manifesting his concern.

"Uh huh! Feeling sleepy, though."

"That's fine! It'll do you good, Wes. Go to it!"

"Say, Art?"

"What?"

"Where's Uncle Jeb? He didn't get back, did he?"

"No, but don't worry, Wes! I'll have him here before you're awake," Artie said more decisively than he was inclined to feel. "Guess you will be O.K. till I get back. I'll leave a lantern lighted."

"Sure, I'll be all right! Feel tired enough to sleep all day to-morrow. Hope you get him back safe!"

"You can bank on it that I will! Now go to sleep!"

"One thing more, Art!"

"Yes?"

Artie, approaching the bunk, saw Westy's face wreathed in smiles and his hand extended. He clasped it, and with a look that told more than words could ever tell, he turned and walked out of the cabin.

With lantern in hand, Artie descended into the gulley walking along cautiously, anxiously looking for some sign or footprint of Uncle Jeb. Coming to the spot where Westy had left him, he found him lying there, burning with fever and delirious.

How he ever succeeded in getting Uncle Jeb back to the cabin, Artie could never quite say. It was nothing more than superhuman effort that came to his aid in getting the sick man up out of the gulley without adding to his discomfort any more than he could help.

Dawn was just beginning to tinge the far horizon with little flecks of light, when Artie half-carried, half-dragged Uncle Jeb into the cabin and laid him in his bunk.

Westy had not awakened, and his quiet, steady breathing bespoke the fact that his slumber was un-broken and nature had once more reasserted itself.

Though his body was utterly weary and his eyes felt weighted down with want of sleep, Artie kept constant vigil by Uncle Jeb's side. He bathed his swollen foot at intervals until the swelling began to gradually diminish.

The hole in his head was what worried Artie most, and he figured that Uncle Jeb, after catching his foot in the bear trap under the elm tree, probably tried with much exertion, to extricate it from the vise that held it, and in his excitement had stepped back further than he was aware. In his fall into the gulley he must have struck his head on a sharp rock.

The only thing to do was to keep the wound clean and wait until Westy had awakened. Then, he could go to the Inn and get the doctor who was stopping there now.

About nine o'clock Westy awoke, refreshed and better. He wanted to go to the Inn himself, seeing the haggard, drawn look on Artie's face, but the tired boy wouldn't hear of it, so he did as he was told and took up the vigil.

When Artie returned from the Inn that afternoon with the doctor, he looked as if he needed medical attention himself and that learned person told him so. But he assured him that sleep was all that he required.

Uncle Jeb was in a delirious state again, as they entered, and his temperature had mounted considerably, so the doctor lost no time in caring for him.

After a while when the fever had subsided somewhat and the sick man had lapsed into a heavy sleep, the doctor turned to attend to Westy's wants. Going about his task he marveled at the courage the boy possessed to have done a thing like that.

That night the physician stayed on, and also the two following nights. The anxious trio were weary and worn with the long waiting, for Uncle Jeb's condition was serious. It was a crucial test for the two young scouts, and they were grieved and filled with apprehension that perhaps they would have to return alone.

The night of the third day there was a change in his condition—for the better. He slept throughout the night, the doctor never leaving his side; likewise the boys.

Then, as the last glittering star in the ethereal firmament faded away, he opened his eyes and gazed weakly, but wide-eyed, around him.

CHAPTER XXXIV

It would be needless to say that hearts were light and voices happy in the little cabin that day. The doctor had just left and assured them that Uncle Jeb was on the fast road to recovery.

When he had disappeared from view, Artie and Westy entered the cabin and sat down to entertain Uncle Jeb with some talk. He asked, for the first time since his illness, just how things had occurred on that near-fateful day. They related in detail all the events and happenings. He smiled with pride at the integrity these two boys had shown.

"I kinda reckon thet it was what you fellas would call a day chuckful o' good turns, eh?" he chuckled.

"I guess that's about it, Uncle Jeb," Westy answered, glad of his old-time good humor returning.

They had planned a while back to camp by the lake for a few days before the summer season was over, and now Uncle Jeb brought up the topic again, and promised them they would go as soon as his strength returned.

It was nearing the end of August and the weather was still very warm, so Artie and Westy received this news with pleasure evidenced in their smiling faces.

"We'll go," said Uncle Jeb, "providin' yuh promise not to take it into yure heads to go a-rescuin' dead eagles!"

"We promise," they both answered with mock-gravity.

They had camped several times out through the different trails west of the cabin, and as a sequel to their recent perilous adventure, they joyously anticipated sleeping so close to it.

That they were two extraordinary boys, Uncle Jeb quietly admitted, for fear seemed utterly foreign to their natures. After their experiences in that region, one would think they would shun the spot, but not Artie and Westy. It lured them on and the old trapper sagaciously told them that, not only were they Boy Scouts of merit, but full-fledged real scouts.

On a bright morning shortly after, they took to the trail in company with the two mules, intending to go on to the Inn before they returned.

They had much to be thankful for, this blithesome trio, swinging along under the glaring sun, without a care in the world. Uncle Jeb after his serious illness seemed to have renewed health once again. He was whistling merrily, by way of expressing himself, and the boys joined in.

With exultant voices echoing throughout the Pass, and back around the lake again, they made camp. Now and then their shouts rang boldly and daringly up toward the hollow and reverberated over the precipice, defying the eagles now from a safe distance. But the day sped onward, crammed full of things to do, and still there was no sign of their erstwhile enemies.

"Wa-al," explained Uncle Jeb, when Westy eagerly asked him if he thought they were liable to nest somewhere else, "it's a-happened afore, thet they go way fer a spell like thet, 'n if we hain't a-seen 'em so fur, 'tain't likely yure a-goin' ter see 'em fer a while longer."

They were sitting cozily content around a bright crackling fire, the stars shimmering overhead and a new moon making its initial bow, as yet just faintly visible in the distant heavens.

Uncle Jeb had been gazing in front of him, his

eyes gradually roving up toward the hollow and around over the Pass. For a moment, it seemed to Westy that he started a little. Then he continued to look again.

"I guess I'm plumb crazy, boys," he began, "but I cud a-swore I seed one o' them durn flashlights afore on thet precipice, movin' back'n forth."

Artie and Westy straightened up, aroused. They knew Uncle Jeb was never given to seeing things. But, to their disappointment, they couldn't discern anything up on the cliff at all. The moon was still in its infancy, and around the hollow and through the Pass one could not penetrate the inky blackness.

"Yit," said Uncle Jeb, as if trying to reason it out with himself, "I'm as shure of it as I kin be, but then thar isn't a pusson aroun' these parts thet would go up on a bet, 'ceptin' you rascals!"

They laughed at the faint hint of admiration that would creep into his voice whenever he referred to the incident.

Resuming his thoughtful preoccupation, they tried to concentrate their vision also, but soon gave it up. Evidently, Uncle Jeb discerned nothing further either, as he arose and yawned sleepily. Putting the fire out they all turned in.

Now Westy, being the romantic and imaginative boy he was, lay rolled in his blankets, gazing fixedly at the stars overhead. The cool night wind caressed his face, as he pondered and turned over in his mind what Uncle Jeb had mentioned about no one around those parts who would dare venture up on the cliff. He suddenly remembered with a thrill the discovery he had made and forgotten about until now. There was no doubt about it, now that he came to think of it again. The day that Artie and he ascended that forbidden trail, the marks were perfectly plain.

Another person had traveled that trail, other than they.

CHAPTER XXXV

GHOSTS

How long he lay awake thinking about this, Westy did not know. In fact, he could not even remember having fallen asleep at all.

He found himself looking above again, wide-awake. In turning around to shift his position facing the lake, he became aware of a pinkish reflection in the sky, just beyond the Pass. He rubbed his eyes and looked again. This time he was sure of it, and saw that it was turning a deeper hue.

What, he thought, could it be? A forest fire? No! He measured the distance of the reflection with his eye, and knew that it wasn't in the mountains. It came to him with a start that it was just about in the direction of the Inn.

Suddenly he arose, quietly, not wanting to arouse the sleepers, should it happen to prove a false alarm.

The capricious moon was now out in all her glory, gleaming down upon the lake and over the cliffs.

Whether her purpose was intentional or not, she seemed deliberately to withold from the narrow Pass even one stray little moonbeam.

Westy tiptoed away, and when he got at a safe margin, he started to run until he got around the lake. Up through the Pass he went, feeling his way securely. Then coming to a rock that would afford him a strong foothold, he clambered up and over the rough stones. There in the distance, sparks shooting into the sky like miniature rockets, was a seething mass of flame. It must be the Inn!

What a terrible situation, he thought!

When Ollie came up to the cabin with their mail, two days ago, he told Uncle Jeb in his quiet blunt way that there were not any guests at the Inn now. There had been an epidemic of scarlet fever among the guests during the past month, and after each stricken one recovered he left. Ol' Pop Burrows was the last one to contract it and still had it in fact, so the remaining guest had taken his leave promptly.

The doctor, who came up from Eagle City every day, forbade Ol' Pop to let any one else come until he was up and around and the place could be thoroughly fumigated. He had inoculated Ollie with some serum or other, as a preventative against the disease, so that he could take care of Ol' Pop without danger of infection.

Ollie went on to say that Ol' Pop wouldn't stay in bed unless he saw the doctor coming, and had insisted on Ollie taking the mail to the cabin regardless of the quarantine. He fairly writhed in anger, with all this "new-fangled bizness o' fumigatin'." He said he didn't care about having any more tourists come that season anyhow, for he had made all the money he wanted to already.

Westy remembered, as he stood there contemplating about it, having heard Uncle Jeb say that Ollie told him all this outside the cabin, beyond their hearing. He still retained his maddening reticence in the presence of the boys.

"So!" Westy exclaimed softly. "They must be there alone, and Ol' Pop still sick! Something will have to be done."

At that moment he had turned in the act of descending, when he saw in the moonlight beyond a form running swiftly toward the Pass. Westy caught his breath and wondered if the form had espied him. In the next second he knew that it had not, for he was invisible in the darkness where

he stood. And he gave thanks to the supercilious
Silver Queen reigning over the heavens that night
for her timely partiality.

He crouched and waited after having climbed
down almost to the trail. Nearer and nearer the
steps came, light and quick, almost panther-like in
action. Finally as a gust of wind would strike one
going past a cavern, so the form rushing past
Westy felt like a stray breeze in that calm night.

Removing his shoes, he started in pursuit of the
fleeing figure. His feet, encountering the sharp
rocks along the way, soon became too bruised to
keep in step with this spooky object. After putting
his shoes back on, he took up the chase once more
as quietly as possible and came at last to the fork
in the trail.

The pursued one went straight up the trail to the
hollow, as though it was thoroughly familiar to him,
never once looking back or stumbling on the way.
He just seemed to be rushing blindly on.

Westy peered from behind a rock and perceived
that the form was not likely to be aware of him now,
for his own individual interests and motives seem-
ingly occupied his whole thought and attention.

So Westy rushed down and around the lake not caring if the figure did see him, for his whole duty now lay in the direction of the Inn.

As he came forward, Uncle Jeb and Artie who were sitting up conversing in low tones, looked at him indifferently.

"Uncle Jeb!" whispered Westy, breathless and excited. "Uncle Jeb! I think that the Inn's on fire!"

"Yuh don't mean to say!" Uncle Jeb gasped in astonishment. "How d'ye know, boy?"

Westy pointed over toward the Pass and there beyond it and overhead was the reflection in the sky, now a flaming scarlet.

"I saw it from the Pass," Westy continued, as if to explain. "I'm perfectly sure of it, Uncle Jeb; that is where it is. And I saw something else in the Pass too——"

Before Westy could finish his story, Uncle Jeb had nudged his arm and pointed above them to the hollow. They all looked and could not repress the chills that ran up and down their spines.

There in the bright light of the moon was the ghost-like figure of a man descending from the precipice into the hollow on a rope!

CHAPTER XXXVI

WESTY CIRCUMVENTS A GHOST?

FOR a few tense moments they stood, staring and unmoved, as if glued to the very spot. The apparition had disappeared within the hollow and it seemed to them that, perhaps after all, it was only a spirit they had seen hovering over the precipice. Suddenly Artie broke the spell.

"Spirits don't generally use ropes, do they?" he asked naïvely, as if he had been thinking it over seriously.

"No, and spirits don't make a noise running through the Pass at night either!" Westy exclaimed. He then explained to them the weird sight he had witnessed. How he had first discovered the figure hurrying in the moonlight beyond, and then gradually becoming enveloped in the darkness, coming through the Pass. "I didn't imagine it either, for I could hear him breathing as he ran past me. When I started after him and we got to the Fork, he went straight up to the cliff!"

Artie was wide-eyed with excitement when Westy revealed to them the possibility of it being a lowly mortal who was causing this furore, but Uncle Jeb listened rather skeptically to the detailed account of this unusual adventure, and preferred believing his own way, irrespective of any other proof, no matter how convincing it might seem.

"I reckon we hain't got no call ter be meddlin' aroun' with ghosts," Uncle Jeb put in. "I guess we jes' better leave him ter his spooky bizness up thar, so long as he hain't hurtin' anything o' ourn. We'll jes' git along pronto ter the Inn!"

Taking his rifle, they started off, Uncle Jeb going it as fast as they. Reaching the Fork, Westy was seized with a most inordinate desire to lag behind a little. He looked longingly up the trail and wondered if he could chance it.

Uncle Jeb and Artie, running along, kept silent so as to keep what strength they had for some later, unseen need. But so preoccupied were they with the shadow of disaster ahead that they were not aware of their missing member.

Westy stood rigid at the Fork as they went on, until he ceased to hear the steady patter of their shoes along the trail. Then, he turned and went up the trail, swiftly but quietly, stepping as much as possible on the moss-covered ground and paying strict attention that he was keeping well out of the limelight.

Breathless, his nerves tingling with the thrilling excitement of the mysterious, he got down flat on his stomach as he made the Cliff. Slowly, ever so slowly, he dragged his body over the cold, rough stones. Directly in the moonlight, he approached the precipice cautiously and looked over.

The hollow was dark and Westy could not see anything to satisfy his curiosity. He listened intently, having covered his nostrils with his handkerchief to muffle the sound of his own breathing. Gradually, he was rewarded. Sounds; some one inhaling as if under intense strain. Then there reached his keen ears the monotonous chip, chip, that a metal instrument would make coming in direct contact with stone.

Whoever it was, thought Westy, they were well within the enclosure, carrying out some dark, hidden purpose in selecting such an hour as this. But what for?

Hadn't Artie been imprisoned in there long enough to know every inch of that dank, gloomy place? He certainly didn't overlook a spot on that smooth surface anywhere in his frenzied attempts to get out.

That something was in the wind was a certainty. Westy resolved then and there to find out what it was before another sun had set upon the horizon. He was never more sure of anything in his whole life than he was right now, that a human being was concerned in all this and not any ghost, as Uncle Jeb would have it.

It wasn't just the sporting thing to do, this fearless scout thought, to be poking into things that perhaps wouldn't turn out to be his affair after all. He chided himself for having let Uncle Jeb and Artie go on unknowingly, and perhaps have to bear the brunt of the danger that was threatening and even at the present moment might have already invaded the Inn.

And so, as he started to draw back as cautiously as he came, his hand came in contact with something rough, just under the weedy growth that sprouted wild between the rocks. Westy stopped and divided the weeds and saw that it was a rope that he had touched. It ran right over the precipice, just as the watchers had seen the figure descend on it. Fate was surely on his side at least, he thought, secretly smiling.

Following the course of the rope he came to a large pine tree, quite a way back on the cliff, where it was tied ever so securely, to the bottom of the trunk. With a deep sigh of satisfaction, he turned and ran pell-mell on down to the Pass and so into the black night again.

His heart contracted with dread when he came stumbling out of the Pass into the open trail once more. There ahead of him was a sight formidable enough to put fear into the heart of any one. It actually looked as though the country around for miles was a seething furnace, the glare in the sky was so great. Westy drew the cool night air into his lungs and started a fresh pace.

Coming nearer and nearer, and at last leaving the mountain trail behind, he took the open road, dashing across fields now and then to save whatever time he could. As he rested for a few precious seconds, almost within calling distance of the Inn, he could feel the force of the heat even there that this raging inferno was expelling over the surrounding countryside. This fact spurred him on considerably, and at last he reached there pretty much out of breath.

The outbuildings were all ablaze and the stable was now a mere memory of its former glory, the crimson embers being the only thing left to identify the spot. One end of the Inn had already caught fire and was in a fair way to continue with fury.

Nothing could be seen of either Artie or Uncle Jeb in the front at all. Darting around to the back, shouting at the top of his voice all the while, he came upon them, also trying to make themselves heard and pounding frantically on the back door. Westy realized why they hadn't heard him, between the deafening roar of the flames and the noise of their own voices.

Uncle Jeb and Artie looked at Westy as though he were a ghost also.

"Wha-ar hev yuh been, lad?" he asked quickly, but with deep concern. "Yuh shure gave us one scare. Never missed yuh 'til we got yonder. Artie 'n I went a ways back agin, 'n cudn't find ye nohow. Jes' got here a minit back, 'n we find all them durn shutters barred from t' inside, 'n both doors bolted too. Nary a one o' them hez answered yit, 'n ye can't git them doors down even with a hatchet."

In their present excitement, Uncle Jeb and Artie forgot about Westy's disappearance, for which he was glad. Time enough for that later, he thought.

The heat was becoming unbearable in the back and, unable to stand it further, they went around to the front again. They went over each individual window on the way around and shook the doors with all their might. Why the windows were shuttered and barred at this time of year Uncle Jeb could not conceive. His anxiety was plainly visible through the deep emotion in his voice. He said they had called at the front and back both until they were hoarse. There wasn't any way that they could break in downstairs. Doors and shutters were both of logs, and even with a hatchet it would take one half the night to make even a dent in one of them. The upper windows were likewise fortified and the frenzied trio stood there helpless, wondering how two people could sleep through all this.

The lower part of the building was built entirely of logs and the upper part of frame. A slate-covered shed over the veranda ran straight up to the bedroom windows in such a way that it would be a difficult thing for one to try and balance himself upon it.

Westy was taking note of all this while Uncle Jeb was talking and he was also thinking fast.

"I can't fer my life know what Ol' Pop's a-thinkin' o', a-barrin' himself in like thet on a hot night. Never knew him ter do it afore 'cept in winter, o' course," Uncle Jeb said, plainly puzzled.

"The whole back is afire now!" exclaimed Artie, who came running around from the side of the Inn.

"Well!" said Westy decisively, as if he had told them in detail before what he contemplated doing. "I'll have to take the nine-hundredth chance, I guess."

"What?" asked Artie excitedly.

"Just give me a boost from the railing, that's all!"

"You're not——" Artie and Uncle Jeb both spoke simultaneously.

Before they finished what they had started to say, Westy had hopped on the porch railing and was making ready to climb the pillar supporting it.

CHAPTER XXXVII

EVIDENCE

ARTIE realized in a flash the seriousness of Westy's intention, and without any further comment gave him a boost up the pillar and onto the shed.

Westy pulled himself up gradually until he was sure that he could stand on his feet with safety. He went around to the side-windows first, trying each only to find they were all barred. With only one more to attempt, he approached it half-fearfully lest it should prove inaccessible too. With trembling fingers he tugged at it and, to his great joy, it yielded.

Artie and Uncle Jeb watched him from below with anxious eyes, beseeching him to be careful and to hurry.

The window was tight shut; locked! But Westy was not to be deterred from his purpose at this time. Raising his knee with determination he struck the glass with a force that sent it crashing into fragments inside. Still there came no sound whatever from within that silent interior.

Stepping through the broken pane into the room he called, but all he could hear was the roar of the flames. The heat in the room was unbearable and he couldn't see very well in the darkness.

He stumbled over one chair and then another. With hands outstretched, he felt something cold. He laughed at the start it gave him for, on examining it closer, he found it to be one of those old-fashioned marble-topped bureaus. It was one of those huge affairs, ample enough to hold the wardrobe of one's entire lifetime. Reaching out into the space around him again, his hand now came in contact with something else; a bed. He could feel the soft covers and knew by its very smoothness that it had been unoccupied that night. Where, he thought, was the door? What room did Ol' Pop use? These and a hundred other thoughts were flashing constantly in his active brain, while he was groping there in the darkness.

If it hadn't been that he knocked the ancient water pitcher and its attendant wash-basin over in his roaming, he probably would have been another half hour trying to find the door. For just after the two articles reached the floor in various pieces Westy shoved his foot ahead of him to kick them aside and in doing so he put his foot on one of the slippery pieces. He landed plunk on the floor, sitting neatly in a pool of water that the pitcher had so recently held. As he sat there so, his eye was just on the level with a little fleck of light, to his right. He put his head over further toward it and his hand out. He felt a door knob revolving under his grasp and knew instantly that the light he had seen was through the keyhole. What joy, what rapture, he thought, as the door swung open under his pressure.

But his ecstasy was of very short duration, for, stepping out into the hall, he saw to his horror the light that he had so joyously perceived through the keyhole wasn't any beacon of safety. It came from the back bedrooms. They were afire! The heat struck his face as he stood there and made it feel blistered.

He stood in the doorway and the light from the burning rooms reflected into the bedroom brightly. Glancing back of him, he saw some towels hanging on a rack above the washstand, whose receptacles he had just demolished. Rushing in, he grabbed a couple of them and stooped, sopping them in the water that had formed a miniature pool on the floor. Taking these, he entered the hall, calling loudly again and ran wildly to the back, one of the towels protecting his face.

He opened one door after the other, but it was unnecessary for him to touch the last door at all. The flames had already destroyed the upper half of it and one could see inside perfectly. They were all practically gone now but yet, it looked to Westy that they had been devoid of any occupants that night, even in the present state of chaos and havoc that this terrible menace had created.

Running to the front again, he opened another one of the bedroom doors. A sickening odor reached him and his heart stood still. Lying on the bed was a form, apparently asleep, outlined against the darkness from the red glare in the back. Westy went over to the bed and bent close. It was Ol' Pop!

The old scout seemed to be hardly breathing at all. In point of fact, it was so faintly and he was lying so rigid and still that Westy realized with a shock he must be unconscious.

Then the flames bursting out into the back of the hall shone through, tingeing the room a scarlet hue.

It provided a sort of arc light and Westy could see Ol' Pop very plain now.

A handkerchief was covering the lower part of his face and Westy gently removed it. As he did so, that nauseating odor permeated the whole room again, and his own nostrils seemed to be filled with it. He raised the piece of muslin to his face.

It had been saturated with chloroform!

CHAPTER XXXVIII

GONE

THE heat was so terrific and the fact that poor Ol' Pop was unconscious made Westy feel a little panic-stricken for the moment. He would try, he thought, getting him down the stairs as gently as possible, if there was yet time.

Pulling back the covers, Westy discovered to his further dismay that the poor old fellow was bound hand and foot to the bed with heavy rope.

"Oh!" exclaimed Westy aloud, thankfully. "The Lord bless my penknife to-night!"

He had a task to do this, for the rope was exceptionally tough and strong. Finally when the last one released the helpless man, Westy tied the wet towel around his head. Then he started in his struggle to remove him, first out of bed and then into the hall.

Reaching the stairs, he saw in consternation that the fire had now taken its toll of these and the whole lower floor also. Suddenly and almost within two feet of them, the flames shot upward from the floor and Westy stepped back quickly. The towel that covered his face was almost dry and his hands and head felt blistered from this fresh onslaught in front of them. Within a second, there was another roar and everything about them in the hall burst into flame. Half dragging his heavy burden, he stepped into the bedroom, which he had previously entered from outside. Just as he slammed the door behind him, there was a terrible, almost deafening roar again. With a terrific crash he could feel the impact of the ceilings and floors giving way.

"Whew," said Westy aloud by the door. "What a piece of luck!"

With another struggle he reached the window and, looking behind him, saw the flames licking their way up the bedroom door. The sight of it made his throat feel so parched that he felt it too was burning. He tried then, to get Ol' Pop out first, but it was no go. Then, just as he was about to call for help, he saw Uncle Jeb climbing up on the shed and Artie behind him.

No word was spoken between them, as they lifted the old man gently out of the window. Artie and Uncle Jeb got down by the porch-railing first with waiting arms outstretched, Westy handed him into their care. As he turned to slide down the pillar, he could see the darting flames leaping out of the window behind him.

They carried the unconscious man a distance away from the intense heat and, laying him down on the soft grass, tried to revive him. Uncle Jeb had found a couple of pails and fetched some water from the spring which had been the source of supply to the Inn. They were busy mopping his face and moistening his lips with the cooling water in their tireless efforts to see some sign of hope on that pale countenance.

Westy looked toward Uncle Jeb sitting quietly there on the ground in the near-dawn. He was gazing at his old friend and there were tears trickling down that weather-beaten visage and his lips were quivering visibly.

It was a sad-looking little company that the breaking day beheld. Huddled on the ground, shivering in the gray chill of early morning, they sat with anxious glances directed toward the still figure lying on the ground blanketed with their coats. Westy and Artie could not suppress the tears brimming in their eyes, from the emotion and pity they felt for Uncle Jeb and the quiet form at their feet.

Almost about to give up hope, the sounds of natural breathing returned in Ol' Pop and they moved nearer joyously. Each taking a hand and rubbing his wrists, they waited anxiously.

Opening his shrewd eyes, he raised his head weakly, but yet showing that the ordeal wouldn't have any further effect on his general health, which was as hardy as any of his type.

He looked toward the smoldering embers, that were the only remnants left of the little rustic Inn, standing just the day before in all its quaint and native beauty. He shook his head sadly, then the dawn of a sudden thought seemed to light in his mind.

"Wa-al, pardner!" he said with a hint of exasperation in his voice. "You 'n I hev lived ter be this age, 'n hed to git fooled fer the fust time in our lives by a tenderfoot. Jes' goes ter show yure never too old ter git kicked!"

"What makes you say that?" Westy asked without being invited, and before either Uncle Jeb or Artie had time to get their breath.

"Fust o' all," continued Pop, ignoring Westy's question. Raising on his elbow he shook his finger with determination. "How 'd ye all git here and git me out 'n the bargain?"

Uncle Jeb acted as spokesman and explained as quickly as possible of Westy's discovery in the sky. He omitted, whether intentionally or not the two boys wondered, mentioning about the ghost.

"Yuh all lissen ter me, 'n I'll tell yer somethin', fer it don't make a bit o' difference now, becuz it's gone by this time anyhow."

"Gone?" they all asked in a chorus.

"Shure ez yure a-sittin' thar all o' ye. My money 's gone every pesky cent. 'N if I hed my way, I'd like ter see thet rascally scoundrel hang fer it. I'd never believed it o' him!"

"Who?" they all asked.

"Ollie!"

CHAPTER XXXIX

THE MAN WITHOUT A SOUL

Uncle Jeb started, they all started in fact, but Ol' Pop seemed oblivious of their evident surprise. Taking a fresh hold with his elbow he continued on, as though his recent statement was nothing extraordinary.

"Ter begin with," he said, "I noticed as how Ollie took ter actin' peculiar-like fer quite a spell back. He kept a-askin' me if I wuz makin' much money 'n if I saved much afore I run the Inn. I'd ketch him every so often lookin' at me funny, but I didn' let myself think much 'bout it. Then, I wuz taken with thet pesky red fever or whatever durn name they give it. Wa-al, when he hears the Doctor say I wuz gittin' better 'n cud git out in a few days, I caught him a-lookin' at me right nasty. After he gits supper he sits aroun' agin eyein' me, 'n it makes me feel so creepy, I go up ter my room ter git clean away frum him. I'm a-sittin' in a rockin' chair a-thinkin' 'bout it and wonderin' what in Sam Hill's

got in ter him. Thar I sit, rockin' back 'n forth by
the winder when I happens ter hear the door creak.
I turn quick and the door is openin' slowly, until
finally it's wide-open. Thar in the doorway stands
Ollie, with thet silly grin what he's hed on him lately.
Not only hez he the grin, but also a gun, which he's
a-pointin' at me, and a rope.

"Fer the minit I think he's gone plumb crazy,
but then I know as how I'm mistakin' in thet, fer
when he starts ter talk, it wuz as natcherell as the
little bit he ever did talk.

"'Ol' Pop Burrows,' sez Ollie, sounding like the
cemetery bell the day thet Sheriff Biggs wuz popped
off by Sly Pete Woozle, 'I'm a-goin' ter make my
get away to-night!'

"'Go ahead!' I sez, 'the better the sooner!' I wuz
thet chilly frum hearin' the spooky voice on him,
I gits all rattled as ter what I wuz talkin'.

"'I intend to!' he sez ag'in, jes' like a funeral
march. 'But not afore yer tells me whar yer keeps
yer swag!'

"'Sufferin' merskeeters!' I sez. 'What's thet?'

"'Yer dough,' he answers.

"I tells him then, thet it wud hev ter be over my
carcass, and he sez jes' like one o' them undertakers,

thet over my carcass it would be, fer he intended sending me West.

" 'Feller,' I sez, tryin' ter be pleasin' 'n thinkin' it may calm his crazy head, 'what foolish talk 'bout sendin' me West. Why, I hain't never been no place else all my life, 'n I got no call ter go now.'

" 'Oh, no, yer ain't never been as fur West as I'll send yer, if yer don't cough up whar the boot is,' he sez, wavin' the gun at me.

" 'O-ho!' I sez, thinkin' I cud kill time. 'So, it's my poor shoes yure after now, eh? Are yer thet hard-hearted as ter leave me in my stockin' feet? Wa-al, thar right on my feet, fer yuh ter take off if yer want. Thar's one thing I kin say though 'n thet is, them soles on the shoes will wear a-hang sight better 'n yourn!'

" 'Yer can't kid me, yuh ol' Shylock!' he sez, orderin' me over ter the bed.

"Then, he sez as how I hez to git in or he'll shoot me. I gits in shure enough 'n he ties me fast ter the bed with the rope. After thet he puts the kivvers over me jes as though it wuz cold weather. He starts shootin' the gun ter the ceilin' 'n tells me he gives me the hull o' five minits ter tell him whar I hide my money. I let four o' the minits go by 'n ez he's a-gettin' ready ter aim, I tells him ez it's up on the Precipice, the haunted one, off o' Eagle Pass, hid in the holler underneath."

Uncle Jeb straightened perceptibly, likewise Westy and Artie. Ol' Pop continued without noticing the surprise they had shown.

"He asks me whar'bouts in the holler 'n I sez the holler is so small he cudn't miss it. I sez thet, thinkin' he'd go and maybe some help wud come in ther meantime frum somewhar. He leaves me then, tied in bed, 'n warns me thet if he doesn't find it he'll kill me when he comes back.

"Wa-al, he went away 'n afore he goes what duz he do but bar all the shutters 'n lock the winders and doors. It seems like he's gone all night 'n I git thet sleepy, I must o' dozed a little. Bye 'n bye, I wake 'n thar he is with the gun 'n madder 'n a hatter. He tells me then thet he's set fire ter my stable 'n soaked everything around with coal-oil. He then sez jes like ez if he wuz doin' me a big favor, thet he intends ter let me burn along with the rest, unless I tell him jes whar'bouts in the holler the money is. At thet minit, I hear the hosses, stomping and whinnying like babies 'n settin' up a terrible fuss. Thet's the only thing what made me tell the rascally scoundrel. Jes for the sake o' them poor hosses."

"I ask him wud he save the hosses shure, if I tell him 'n he sez yes. But instead o' thet he laughs after I tell and sez as how he hez no intention o' savin' the hosses ner me neither. Laughin' jes like a maniac, he takes a handkerchief outer his pocket 'n a bottle 'n when he pours the stuff outer it he sez, 'Here's how, yuh ol' miser!' Thet's the last I remember 'n ever want to 'bout Ollie Baxter. Yuh kin bet he's found the money 'n we'll never see him ag'in!"

"I don't know about that!" Westy interposed smilingly. The sun was rising in the east and the day was beginning to take on her mantle of light in real earnest now.

"What do yer mean, son?" asked poor Ol' Pop sadly.

"Yes, what do you mean, Wes?" Artie and Uncle Jeb both asked curiously.

"He got into the hollow sure enough and I guess he found the money all right, but he'll never get out unless one of us goes there to get him out!" Westy said mysteriously.

"Why?" interrogated the voices in unison.

"Because I cut the rope!"

CHAPTER XL

OLLIE MAKES HIS EXIT

WHEN Ol' Pop felt up to it they started back for Eagle Pass to breakfast. He was talking with Uncle Jeb and said he hadn't decided what he would do for a while and would stay in the cabin while he was thinking it over. Anyhow, he mentioned that if his money was still intact, he could live the rest of his life in comfort.

Westy and Artie walking ahead could hear them talking and wondered then why Ol' Pop had risked his money to such a place as the hollow! Not only his money, but it had almost cost him his life, they thought, and all for what?

Undoubtedly if we could answer questions like those, we would have to be infinite in our wisdom.

However, the two old scouts praised these two young scouts for their intuitive sense concerning Ollie, and vowed that they would never again think they were too old to learn something from these younger minds.

HE KEPT THE RIFLE POINTED DIRECTLY AT HIM, AS ARTIE
STRUGGLED WITH THE HEAVY STEEL BOX.

Westy Martin in the Rockies. *Page* 189

As they rounded the lake they all glanced simultaneously up toward the hollow with eager eyes. There was Ollie, who had spied them as soon as they appeared at the lake, leaning over the edge waving to them frantically for help. Westy remarked that he thought it was just the thing he would do. A coward when he was cornered.

They sat there joyously eating breakfast, watching his frenzied appeals for help. It was Westy who had suggested letting him suffer at least apprehension, if they couldn't make him suffer anything else. Any one so devoid of human feeling as this stone-faced individual deserved the full limits of the law, he concluded.

"I told you from the looks of his eyes he didn't have any soul!" Artie said proudly.

"Wa-al, boys," Uncle Jeb said, "it wuz shure left fer you 'uns ter show us, wuzn't it?"

"I hope you won't believe the hollow is haunted any more?" Westy asked Uncle Jeb.

"No, indeedy, not now!" he said, chuckling, and then turned to Ol' Pop. "How cum, yer ol' crony you, thet ye picked thet durn place ter hide yer money?"

"Cuz," answered Ol' Pop, not very informative,

"I didn' believe in any fool ghosts, 'n you 'n all the folks here'bouts did."

After breakfast, when they got good and ready, Westy and Artie started off around the lake, feeling for all the world like two officials of the law. Westy, in the lead going up the Cliff trail, had Uncle Jeb's rifle nonchalantly slung over his left shoulder. No matter how indifferently placed it looked to the beholder, Westy was perfectly aware of its exact position, for it took him at least five minutes to get it placed in the right position, just as he wanted it. Artie had a club in his hand that looked rather primitive in design, but nevertheless he felt that it was a weapon of defense at least.

Reaching the precipice cautiously, these two boy scouts made sure they were unheard before they approached the enemy.

Ollie was too busy concentrating his gaze toward the lake and didn't see or hear them coming.

"Hands up!" Westy commanded authoritatively. "Hand the money over quick or I'll blow your brains out!" He was now waving the rifle menacingly back and forth between Ollie's little eyes.

"You mean throw the money up, don't you, Wes?" Artie said in a very un-official tone.

Westy gave Artie a black look that rather told him how unseemly his remark had been.

"Of course, that's what I did say!" he lied gallantly to save his face.

"What youse kids trying to do, scare me?" Ollie said in the east-side vernacular and with a show of bravado. "Youse haven't a chanct in the woild!"

"Is that so!" exclaimed Westy and more for something further to say than anything else continued, "Your old friends, the bulls, are just coming up the trail now with a nice pair of bracelets for you. Are you going to throw that money box up here?"

"I can't!" said Ollie, visibly pale. "It's too heavy."

"Very well," said Westy, master of the situation at once. "I'll hand you the rope and you can tie it around the box, so we can haul it up."

"Aw-right!" said Ollie, his teeth chattering now. "Are the bulls there now?"

"Coming!" said Westy.

He kept the rifle pointed directly at him, as Artie struggled with the heavy steel box coming over the precipice. When it had landed safely, Artie carried it back a way on the Cliff. Westy, his curiosity aroused, drew back from the precipice to look at the incentive of all the trouble. He and Artie were conversing in low tones about the weight of the box.

"Say, Wes," asked Artie very softly, "what made you say that?"

"About the bulls?"

"Yes."

"Oh, I don't know. I just hit the nail on the head too. I suppose though it must have been my own common sense told me that Ollie was a criminal before, or he wouldn't have done such a low, despicable thing to poor Ol' Pop."

Whether Ollie Baxter thought that the bulls had finally arrived on the scene is a question. Westy has always thought so anyway, and we are inclined to believe him. He claims that Ollie must have become panic-stricken, mistaking his and Artie's low converse for the bulls.

At any rate, be that as it may, there was a sudden cry as of fright, and by the time Westy and Artie got to the end of the precipice and looked over, Ollie Baxter was plunging in mid-air through that vast space and hence into Eagle Lake.

CHAPTER XLI

SKELETONS

WHEN Westy and Artie reached the lake bearing the heavy steel-box with Ol' Pop's life-savings intact, Uncle Jeb and his old pardner were scanning the surface of the lake with all their might.

Westy set the box down and Ol' Pop took his hand and his voice shook with emotion and the deep gratitude he felt for this boy who had rendered him such help.

"Don't know how I'm a-goin' ter pay yer back!" he said. "Guess nothin' I cud give yer wud be worth what I owe yer, but I kin tell yer pronto, boy, yure good-stuff 'n never will I forget ye as long as I live!"

Westy felt well repaid in having him just talk like that. Indeed it made him feel shy and embarrassed to have this hardy old pioneer condescend to a lowly boy scout such as he. He tried to tell Pop as best he could that he wanted no pay of any kind, and that he had done no more than any boy should do.

Leaving Ol' Pop to his wealth Uncle Jeb and the boys started around the lake.

"Did you notice the exact spot he jumped in, Uncle Jeb?" Westy asked.

"As fur as I cud see, he landed right about thar!" Uncle Jeb explained, pointing his finger toward the spot he meant. "He wuz a-comin' on down thet fast, turnin' somersaults all the way, thet it made me right dizzy ter watch him. He landed with a thump 'n I reckon he never did cum up agin, he went down thet fast."

"Well, I have a good mind to take a plunge and do a little investigating myself," Westy said enthusiastically.

"Go to it!" Artie said heartily.

"Be careful, boy!" Uncle Jeb warned him. "Yuh've hed yure share o' narrow escapes already!"

"I will!" called Westy, making the plunge.

He swam around for a while and, finding no trace of anything, returned to the shore.

All that day they kept watch, but nothing revealed itself from the lake. Night came and they sat around the campfire once more, warmed in soul as well as body, that they were all sitting there safe and sound.

Westy and Artie were voicing their regrets that the summer had gone so quickly.

Events of the night before were gone over again, and, as the last spark of the fire died out on that pebbly shore, Westy rolled into his blankets, face upturned to the starry skies once again. They were to return to the cabin in the morning and he wanted to fix in his mind forever the beautiful spectacle that surrounded him, revealing all its naked beauty to his wondering eyes.

The stars overhead in that dark blue sky, shimmering and twinkling down upon him, seemed to want to confide in him the mystery of the heavens. The mountains around, so frowning and formidable in aspect to most people, looked to Westy that night majestic and serene, a solid wall of protection to mankind. Everything around him in fact that night brought gladness to his heart for he was happy in the thought that he had been of benefit to his fellowbeings.

And so musing, sleep seemed utterly to have deserted him and he felt not the least need of any.

"Well," he whispered softly, "this is the last night under the stars, so I might as well make the most of it. Guess I'll paddle around and finish my dreaming out here while I'm at it!"

He entered the canoe noiselessly and pushed off, lapping the water lightly with the paddle, seeming hardly to have touched it at all.

The fact that a tragedy had entered the lake that day, did not make Westy fear it at night. What he was not afraid of living, he surely wouldn't fear dead.

His thoughts drifting lazily along and with his dreamy eyes fixed on Her Majesty, the Moon, he felt something strike the canoe.

The impact felt no more than what a small log would in striking it, but nevertheless Westy, always observing, looked.

It was mentioned before that Westy did not know what fear was. To retract it a little it can be here recorded, that he did receive quite a shock at first when he looked over the side of the canoe.

There floating in the water, directly in the moonlight, was the skeleton of a man and a few yards away from that—was another.

CHAPTER XLII

THE LOST IS FOUND

THIS time Westy uttered a cry, even if only one of surprise, but still a cry and it awakened the little slumbering camp.

He had paddled back to shore by the time Uncle Jeb and Artie reached there. Telling them of his discovery, they jumped into the canoe and went back to the spot. The skeletons were still floating there all right and with the aid of their paddles the boys succeeded in pushing the spooky-looking things onto shore.

Needless to say another night was lost in which to sleep, but they were in no mood to lie down in peaceful slumber after looking at anything like that. Lying on the shore side by side in the yellow moonlight, they were a weird and ghastly sight.

Westy bent down and saw that around the neck of one was an object of some kind. He touched it carefully and then again. Taking out his trusty pen-knife, he cut the string that held it, not caring to touch the poor creature with his bare hands.

As it came off, and Westy held it up, he saw to his surprise that it was an oil-skin wallet. No wonder it had stayed intact while the flesh of its owner had deteriorated into nothingness!

He held it up in the light while Uncle Jeb and Artie gathered around him. It was air-tight all right and Westy found, when he finally got it open, that it contained papers; probably some important, official documents, they thought.

While the moon was bright it was not light enough to see clearly and so be able to read them.

When morning came and breakfast was finished, Westy brought the papers out. The writing was pretty unintelligible now, but still Westy could make out words here and there. He gasped with astonishment and read aloud to his dumbfounded listeners.

Mr. John Temple's name was mentioned, as representing a certain railroad, and giving him the right of way over a certain tract of ground belonging to one Ezra Knapp, for a given consideration. It all ran along those lines and there was at least enough decipherable to know what it was all about.

"It's the agreement!" exclaimed Uncle Jeb, "thet Mr. Temple felt so bad over losing!"

"Then——" before Artie could finish Westy broke in.

"They must be the skeletons of the lost surveyors!"

How those poor men met their death in that watery grave is not known, probably never will be, but it is a certainty, as Westy remarked, that no matter how useless Ollie Baxter's life may have been, his death was timely and for some good purpose.

Westy figured that the force of Ollie's body in striking bottom must have disturbed those two skeletons, lying there through all those years, sending them floating to the top, while his remained on bottom.

At any event Ollie Baxter has never been seen again, but he surely did Westy a good turn in doing what he did.

They telegraphed from Eagle City the next day, to Mr. Temple, of Westy's wonderful find.

It meant great rejoicing to Mr. Temple and before he left Bridgeboro for the West, he called on Westy's father.

He told Mr. Martin what a big thing it had been for his son to have unearthed the agreement.   He went on to say that it meant one of the biggest business deals of the day and that they would surely have to reward him.

Mr. Martin said he spoke for Westy and knew that his son wouldn't think of any such thing, but was only too happy to have rendered Mr. Temple that service.

After Mr. Temple had left, promising to bring the boys safely back with him, Mrs. Martin looked at her husband, eyes gleaming with pride.

"With all your shouting," she said smilingly, "about that boy's romanticism and lack of business ideas he's proven himself a bigger and better business man than you are!"

"My dear!" said Mr. Martin with good-humor, "don't rub it in! I know when I'm licked!"

One morning, a few days later, Westy and Mr. Temple stood looking up toward the precipice. The older man was telling this wonder-scout that everything was settled and in readiness to continue where they had to leave off ten years ago. The cliff, he told him, with its little tragic hollow would be dynamited within the next two months to make way for the interests of bigger and better business.

"So, what do you think of your accomplishments, Westy?" Mr. Temple asked, waving his hand over toward the Pass and then to the Cliff.

"Well," replied Westy, smiling, "I guess that's that!"

THE END

This Isn't All!

Would you like to know what became of the good friends you have made in this book?

Would you like to read other stories continuing their adventures and experiences, or other books quite as entertaining by the same author?

On the *reverse side* of the wrapper which comes with this book, you will find a wonderful list of stories which you can buy at the same store where you got this book.

Don't throw away the Wrapper

Use it as a handy catalog of the books you want some day to have. But in case you do mislay it, write to the Publishers for a complete catalog.

THE WESTY MARTIN BOOKS
By PERCY KEESE FITZHUGH
Author of the "Tom Slade" and "Roy Blakeley" Books, Etc.

**Individual Colored Wrappers. Illustrated.
Every Volume Complete in Itself.**

Westy Martin, known to every friend of Roy Blakeley, appears as the hero of adventures quite different from those in which we have seen him participate as a Scout of Bridgeboro and of Temple Camp. On his way to the Yellowstone the bigness of the vast West and the thoughts of the wild preserve that he is going to visit make him conscious of his own smallness and of the futility of "boy scouting" and woods lore in this great region. Yet he was to learn that if it had not been for his scout training he would never have been able to survive the experiences he had in these stories.

WESTY MARTIN

WESTY MARTIN IN THE YELLOWSTONE

WESTY MARTIN IN THE ROCKIES

WESTY MARTIN ON THE SANTA FE TRAIL

WESTY MARTIN ON THE OLD INDIAN TRAILS

GROSSET & DUNLAP, *Publishers,* NEW YORK